Praise for
Fire Pony

"Rodman Philbrick's gripping cowboy story with menace, *Fire Pony*, reads like John Steinbeck."
The Sunday Times

"A compelling page-turner... You cannot fail to become emotionally involved with this story."
Write Away

"Gripping."   *Disney's Big Time*

"Totally engaging and often very touching... With its echoes of various timeless American cowboy stories, this is a novel with all the makings of a classic in its own right."   *Books for Keeps*

"The tension will hook readers till the dramatic conclusion."   *Booklist*

"Full of warmth, humanity and interesting detail."
School Librarian Journal

"This book is a must-read... Philbrick is one of the most brilliant and compelling living American children's writers. Enjoy!"
...land Magazine

FIRE PONY

RODMAN PHILBRICK

USBORNE

Look Beyond the Story...

Turn to the back of the book for insights and interviews with the author

This edition first published in the UK in 2008 by Usborne Publishing Ltd.,
Usborne House, 83-85 Saffron Hill, London EC1N 8RT, England.
www.usborne.com

First published in the UK in 2005. Text copyright © Rodman Philbrick, 1996.
Published by arrangement with Scholastic Inc., 557 Broadway, New York, NY 10012, USA.
Cover copyright © Usborne Publishing Ltd., 2008.

A CIP catalogue record for this book is available from the British Library.

JFMAMJJASON /07
ISBN 9780746090831
Printed in Great Britain.

For everybody who's ever been thrown
from a horse and got back on.

Catch a Sight of Heaven

1

"We'll just keep moving," Joe Dilly says to me. "Pick up a job here and there. Anybody looks at us cross-eyed, we hit the road. You with me on this, little brother?"

I go, "Sure, Joe, I'm with you," even though inside I'm still pretty worried about all the bad stuff catching up.

We're coming down from the high mountains in that old Ford pickup truck with the camper back, and Joe's whistling and tapping his hands on the wheel, like he don't care if the cops want to talk to him about that fire back in Montana.

"Look around," he says, pointing out the window. "It'll help put your mind at ease."

He's right. It's hard to stay worried when every turn in the road there's something brand-new to look at. Trees so high you can't see the tops, and sometimes these open pastures that roll right on down to the edge of the world.

All of a sudden – *bang!* – that old right front tyre blows out like a gunshot and I'm hanging on for dear life with the truck bucking and heaving like an unbroken horse. And Joe Dilly, well, you never heard nobody can curse like Joe Dilly when he's in the mood.

He finally manages to wrestle the truck over to the side of the road, near this thick stand of tall trees, and you can tell how the mountain drops away real steep right under those trees.

"Just step aside," Joe Dilly says, rubbing his hands together. Like he's almost happy that tyre blew, like it was an adventure he'd planned on having, for the fun of it. He's going, "Make way for Mr. Fix-It," and "Okay, partner, just you watch while I make this little old truck levitate," the way he always talks to himself when he's working.

Pretty soon he's got the truck jacked up and the bad tyre is lying there like a chunk of roadkill, and I'm kind of wandering along by the edge of the road, looking to catch a peek at whatever critters are hiding in the dark shadowy places under those tall trees.

"Hey, Joe!" I go. "Are there mountain lions round here?"

He looks up from where he's spinning the tyre wrench. "Mountain lions?" he says. "You bet your bottom dollar, sports fans! This here is mountain lion country."

"You ever shoot a lion, Joe?"

He gives me that flinty, squinty look of his, and then he winks and goes, "Nah. Saw one once, coming over the ridge."

"What'd you do?"

"Ran like a man on fire," he says, and then he's back whistling and working.

I keep following along the side of the road and suddenly there's this gap in the trees and you can see all the way down the mountain into this big, golden valley.

Something about that valley, the way it seems all glowy and filled with light, it makes my heart thump hard against my ribs. It's almost as if I'm afraid to take another breath or blink my eyes or it'll be like something you see in a dream, something really special that fades away as soon as you wake up, and then you can't remember why it was so important.

I sing out, "Joe! Come here and look at this!"

"Whatcha got, a big old lion? Probably a tree stump looks like a lion."

"I catched a sight of heaven, Joe!"

Which gets his attention. Before I know it, Joe Dilly is standing right behind me, looking over the top of my head, and his voice changes and gets real quiet.

"I'll be darned," he says. "And look there, off to the south. I spy a ranch."

"I can't see it," I say.

"There."

He points far off, and now I can see the glinting where the sunlight hits off the metal roofs. There's a lot of barns and outbuildings, and a bigger, sprawling place must be the main ranch house. And you can see the dark little speckles moving over the floor of the valley, if you look hard enough.

"Horses, Joe. I see horses."

"Yep," says Joe. "Horses."

The way he says it, you know that horses are his favourite kind of critters, and that includes most people.

"Can we go there, Joe?" I say. "You think we're far enough from Montana?"

I'm hoping maybe this time things will work out. That's when I feel both his hands on my shoulders, and Joe gives me a little squeeze. He says, "Tell you what, Roy. We'll give her a look. We can do that much."

"It sure is pretty," I say.

He's quiet for a minute and then he goes, "Lots of things look pretty from this far off."

2

The Bar None, Everybody Welcome

Joe says it's bad luck to drive onto a place before we've been properly welcomed, so he parks the truck outside the gate and we walk in on our own steam.

The first thing I notice is this big old sign that hangs over the entrance. It says THE BAR NONE, and under it is this other sign that says "Everybody Welcome".

"The Bar None," I say. "What's that supposed to mean?"

"Some kind of joke, I guess," Joe says. "People put the funniest names on ranches sometimes. Before I come to get you, I worked this place once in Arizona called itself 'Egg Ranch'. Well, I asked 'em what did they raise, was it horses or eggs? And it turns out the man owned the place, his real name was Egg."

"You're pullin' my leg," I say.

"I swear," says Joe Dilly. "Thomas Egg, that was his name."

You never know with Joe, not from his face – it could be the real truth, or he's having fun.

When he first showed up and took me away from that crummy foster home, I believed everything he said. I'd always pretended my big half-brother Joe was gonna come and rescue me, and then he did. Once he told me the world was flat and we'd fall off the other side if we didn't have Super Glue on our feet, and I believed him. Another time he said if you fart and sneeze at exactly the same instant, you'll explode, and I believed that, too.

I was littler then, that's my excuse, but pretty soon I figured out that with Joe Dilly you have to take everything he says with a dose of salts, or catch him winking, because he will try to fool you now and then. So maybe there really is a guy named Thomas Egg and maybe there ain't.

Anyhow, like I say, we're walking up that long driveway on our own steam, it must be near a mile from where we left the truck to the first stable, that's the scale of things at the Bar None. Just the two of us kicking up dust, and the smell of horses in the air, which ain't a bad smell.

We don't know what's waiting for us at the end of the road, but somehow I've got this feeling it'll be okay.

The first person we see is this Mexican-looking guy about Joe's age, he's leaning on the fence rail watching these horses trot round and round inside this big corral. They're all Arabians, so beautiful and silky the way they move it makes you feel out of breath just watching.

The Mexican, he gives us a little wave with his hat and Joe goes over to him and says, "That sign of yours mean what it says?"

"I guess," says the Mexican. His eyes are jumping from Joe to me. He looks pretty friendly, but you can tell he's not ready to make up his mind about us, one way or the other.

"Everybody welcome," Joe says.

"That's what it says, all right. Mr. Jessup, he put that up himself."

Joe nods. "Uh huh. I take it Mr. Jessup is the owner."

"Yep," says the Mexican. "He's the owner and I'm the foreman. What can I do for you?"

"Nothin' special," says Joe. He reaches out and gives

my head a rub for luck like he does. "Got any horses need shoeing, or their hoofs trimmed, I'm your man."

"Oh?" You can tell the way he says it the Mexican ain't interested, but he stays polite. "Sorry, there's already a fella takes care of that." He squints at me and I can see where he'd like to smile, but he's holding back. "Now, you care to stay for lunch, we put on a real good feed."

Joe Dilly's smiling in a way that'll make you nervous, if you dare look him in the eye. "We ain't looking for no handout," he says, his voice getting real cool and flat. "I'm the best damn shoer that ever fit an iron to a hoof."

"I don't doubt it," the Mexican says. "But Mr. Jessup does all the hiring, and he's gone for a spell. Won't be back for a week or more."

Joe Dilly takes a deep breath and then he stands a little closer and says, "There a horse nobody can get near? I mean a real spooked animal won't be touched. The kind of outlaw horse will kick any man tries to get close. You got an animal like that, by any chance?"

The Mexican shrugs. "Sure we do," he says. "Bound to, on a spread this big."

Joe goes, "There's never been a horse born I couldn't turn." Then he says, "Tell you what. If I can fix the baddest animal you got, we'll take a meal with you and call it even."

"No need for that," says the Mexican.

"That's the deal," says Joe Dilly, and the way he says it, you know that's final.

The Mexican, he looks at the both of us, and after a while he nods. "Okay," he says. "Let's see what you can do with Showdown."

3
Showdown Says Hello

I wait there with the Mexican while Joe goes back to fetch the truck. The Mexican turns out to be a real nice guy – his name is Rick Valdez, and he's not from Mexico at all.

"I was born right here on the Bar None," he tells me, "only that was before Mr. Jessup bought the place."

"I sure like to watch them Arabians," I say.

"Yep, I noticed that," Rick says, and when he smiles you never saw teeth so white. "Is that your dad?" he asks, looking out where Joe Dilly has walked off.

I tell Rick that Joe's my big brother, we had the same mother but different fathers, and Rick says, real casual,

"Is that so? Where you boys from? Not these parts, I guess."

"Oh, we're from all over," I say, which is exactly what Joe tells me to say, if anybody asks, because you never know what might be catching up on us.

"All over," says Rick.

"Here and there." I point quick to a high-stepping Arabian that's sauntering by, showing off how light and fine she is. "Sure is a pretty horse," I say.

"We've got about two hundred more that's just as pretty," Rick says. "So your big brother, he looks after you, is that it?"

I smile and nod, but really I'd rather just watch them Arabians on parade, because Joe takes a nervous fit whenever anybody gets to asking a lot of personal-type questions. And Rick, he backs off and talks about the weather and the horses and stuff, and I ask him how many mountain lions he's seen and he tells me he's never seen one at all, but that doesn't mean they aren't up there.

"They blend in," he says. "You think it's a yellow rock, but really it's a cougar keeping still. That's what we call 'em in these parts, cougars."

"What about grizzly?" I ask. "Could a grizzly beat a mountain lion? I mean a cougar?"

"Now that would be a fight," he says. "Bear is bigger

but the cat might be quicker. Let me think on that."

Before Rick can tell me any more about bears and mountain lions, Joe comes back with the truck and he's all business, rubbing his hands together and smiling with just his teeth. "Showdown," he says. "Ain't that a card game?"

"He's no game," says Rick, leading the way. "I want you to be real careful. Mr. Jessup hears somebody got busted up by a horse that belongs to him, he won't be happy."

"I'll be careful," Joe says. "I'm the carefullest man alive." And he's winking at me, because if they had a contest for the *least* carefullest man alive, Joe Dilly would win, hands down.

What happens next is Joe backs up to one of the big stable buildings, and he sets out his portable forge, where he can heat up the irons and bend 'em to fit perfect. We're getting low on propane, but Joe guesses there's enough left for one more job.

Rick the foreman, he's standing there watching, and when Joe has the forge hot enough to work, he says, "You get a shoe on Showdown and you'll be the first. Last man got in the stall with that horse, it was all we could do to get him out alive."

"Don't worry about that," Joe says. "You gonna show me this killer horse, or what?"

"It's your funeral," Rick says. He forces a laugh but you can tell he's worried.

Joe, he's whistling and grinning and you'd think he was cooking up some breakfast, not iron horseshoes for some critter that might be crazy enough to kill him if he's not real careful. I make like I'm not nervous, but it's a fib, really, because my stomach is all clenched up and my face hurts from pretending to smile.

Joe Dilly, he follows Rick into the stable and I hang back a ways, like they told me. It's pretty dark inside, until your eyes get used to it, and the smell of hay and oats and horses and leather fills up the air. It's a fresh smell, though, so you know there's a whole lot of spit polish and elbow grease goes into keeping these stables mucked out.

"Mr. Jessup figured Showdown would be a project," Rick says, "but it ain't worked out. Sometimes you get bad blood in a Thoroughbred and there's nothing you can do to fix it. Most owners would have had him put down, or shipped off, but not Mr. Jessup, he can't stand to put a horse down, even if it's for the best."

The way he says that, it makes me like Mr. Jessup, even though I never seen him.

I'm starting to see better in the soft, dim light, and

I can tell where we're headed. There's a box stall off to the side, away from the others. The steel gate has a good-sized bar across it instead of just a latch, and the gate is all pushed out from the inside, where it's been kicked. The horse in there, he's backed up in the shadows like he don't want to be looked at. Or maybe because he wants a running start at that gate.

"Say hello, Showdown," Rick says.

That sets him off and the next thing you know – *wham!* – a hoof smashes the gate about head high – and there's Showdown, with his black eyes blazing like crazy marbles and his nostrils flaring like his tail's on fire. He's showing us the whites of his eyes, and all of his teeth, and the first thing I figure, you give an apple to that horse, he'll take your whole hand.

"No halter on him," Joe says. "He keep tearing it off, does he?"

"We about gave up on a halter," Rick says. "He'd get to rubbing his head against the stall till he drew blood, or wore out the leather, and that's no good."

"Okay," Joe says. "You two back off, give us some breathing room. Me and Showdown are going to have a little talk."

"I don't know about that," Rick says.

"We'll be fine," Joe says, and he won't take no for an answer.

So me and Rick wander over to the other side of the barn where the light comes pouring in and you can see all those fine Arabians frolicking around in the corral like they're having a party. Sometimes you get the impression them Arabians are more like dogs than horses, they're so playful and friendly, and so tolerant of human people.

"Your brother really know what he's doing?" Rick asks me, keeping his voice low. "It's not worth getting hurt just to prove a point."

"He's real good," I say.

"I sure hope so," Rick says, but he's talking to himself, not to me.

I'm worried but not *too* worried, because Joe Dilly's never been hurt bad by a horse, not on purpose. On the other hand, you never know, do you?

Rick and me are leaning in the barn door, not saying a lot, and we've got our ears cocked, but it's real quiet; all you can hear is the murmur of Joe Dilly's voice, sounds like soft water in a shallow stream, and if you keep listening you'll start to drift off, it makes you feel calm and good.

Which is what it does to Showdown, I guess, because when we wander back to take a look, Joe's all the way inside the stall with that crazy-acting Thoroughbred, and he's stroking that horse real gentle and the horse is sighing and making little whinny noises like it wants to talk, and maybe it *is* talking, only you'd have to be Joe Dilly to understand.

"Well I'll be damned," Rick says. "It's a miracle."

That's what a lot of folks think, the first time they see Joe work a bad horse, but he says it ain't no miracle, it's just a gift he has, and he don't understand it neither.

4

Here Comes Trouble

So Joe Dilly gets hired on at the Bar None, and he's in such a fine mood almost two weeks go by and he ain't got in trouble yet.

"This time it'll be different," he keeps telling me. "I can feel it. Must be I turned over a new leaf, because something about this place agrees with me."

"You mean we're gonna stay put?" I ask.

"For the time being," Joe says. "Unless you'd rather we hit the road, see what's over the next mountain."

"I like it here," I say, maybe too quick, but Joe doesn't mind, he's in such a rare mood, almost like he was a different person. And for a while there I'm thinking maybe he really *has* shook loose of the

24

crazies that got us run off that ranch in Montana, and kept us moving on from place to place, with maybe something catching up, like he's always saying.

'Course I was wrong. Joe Dilly is Joe Dilly, even if he don't act it on the outside.

* * *

The best thing about working the Bar None is they give us a little bunkhouse all to ourselves. I ask Rick if real cowboys used to sleep in this old bunkhouse and he says depends on what you mean by cowboys.

"This never was a cattle ranch," he says. "From the beginning, it was horses. When I was your age we rounded up herds of quarter horses, and some mustang, but we never did drive no cows."

He's just being fussy, because the way I see it, you don't have to herd cows to qualify as a cowboy, and I already seen Rick working them Arabians, and he's good enough to be in a rodeo. He can't calm a crazy horse like Joe Dilly can, but he sure can ride.

Every morning there's chores to be done, like always. Rick says even Hercules couldn't muck out all the stalls on the Bar None, but I sure wish he'd give it a try – I'd be happy to watch him, and offer advice.

Okay, the truth is that mucking out them stalls ain't

all that bad, but the chore I like best is helping Joe. There's near about two hundred horses on the Bar None, and more always getting bought or sold or traded. Every day there's some need to have their hooves trimmed up, or get new shoes fitted, so there's more work than any one man can handle by himself.

* * *

One morning we're out by the main corral, checking what horses need fixing, when Joe says, "The most important thing about a horse is does it feel right on its feet – without good feet, you ain't got a good horse, period. You got to work a horse from the ground up."

He's told me this lots of times before, but I don't let on. You want to learn things, sometimes you got to keep your trap shut.

"Pay attention now, Roy. You with me?"

"I'm with you, Joe."

"Well that's fine. Okay, you have to start by using your eyes. You watch that horse walking, and see does it have knock-knees, or bowlegs, or does it forge or scalp."

I already know some things. A horse that forges, the hind feet clip at the backs of the front feet, and if you don't fix it, the horse will come up lame, or worse.

Your scalping horse, that means the front hooves kind
of click together as it walks, and you can fix that, too,
if you know what you're doing.

"Let me take a look at that one," Joe says, and he
means this trail horse called Slow Hand.

Slow Hand, he's pretty friendly, and I manage to get
a halter on him and bring him out of the corral. The
first thing with a horse, I'll walk it around some and Joe
will study it and study it, and sometimes he ambles
over and runs a hand along the shoulder or the cannon
bone – just the touch will tell him what ails that horse.

"You got him, do you?" he asks.

"I got him," I say.

Slow Hand, he's feeling frisky, pulling at the halter
and jerking his head like they will, and Joe is crouched
down in his leather apron, and you can tell he's seeing
something he don't like.

"Back that horse up," he says.

Easy to say, but you just try backing up a nine-
hundred-pound animal when you're as small as me!
Joe don't say nothing, he waits until I get the horse
moving the way he wants, and then he nods and says,
"That poor animal can't feel his feet. Bet you a dollar
some darn fool cut the frogs away."

Most people, they hear the word "frog", they think
it lives in a pond, but there's part of a horse's hoof they

call a frog, and Joe is very particular about the way it gets trimmed. Sure enough, he lifts up the rear leg and checks the bottom of the hoof, and if I'd been fool enough to take the bet, he'd have my dollar by now.

"Don't you worry," he says to Slow Hand. "We'll fix you right up." Then he strokes the horse, and pats it a certain way, and the next thing you know, he's pulling off the old shoes and filing away at the hoof until he's got it bevelled the way he wants.

A horse's hoof, it's like a great big toenail, only thicker and stronger, and you got to keep it trimmed right or the whole animal suffers. There's a science to it, Joe says, and he's teaching me a little bit at a time.

"A horse thinks with its feet," he says. He's bending over, filing away at that hoof, and you can see how his hands are gentle and strong at the same time. "All them nerves connect up to the brain, of course, but it starts right here where the animal touches the ground. A good horse'll feel a train coming long before you hear the whistle, and that's a fact."

I've got Slow Hand by the halter, like you're supposed to, but even if I wasn't there to hold him steady, that horse wouldn't move. Not with Joe Dilly working his feet.

When Joe gets done, Slow Hand is like a brand-new horse, and he runs around that big corral showing off and demonstrating how good he feels. And Rick, he's watching everything Joe does and he's just as pleased as punch.

"Where you been all my life?" he says to Joe. "One of these days I'm going to pull off these old boots and let you fit horseshoes to me."

"Sure," says Joe. "Any time you like."

"One of these days," Rick says, laughing. "But not today."

Right about then I notice this lady I never seen before, she's coming out by the row of cabin houses where most of the Bar None ranch hands live with their families, and I swear, she's looking right at me, like she knows exactly who I am.

Joe says, "Who's that?"

"I forget her name," Rick says, kind of uneasy all of a sudden. "Works for the county."

"Is that a fact?" says Joe. "What is she, a tax collector?"

Before Rick can answer, the lady, she's kind of Indian-looking with dark eyes and big silver earrings, anyhow she comes over and shakes Joe's hand.

"Pleased to meet you," she says. "I'm Sally Red Dawn."

You never seen nobody less interested in making her acquaintance than Joe Dilly, but it's too late to skedaddle, so he just says, "Is that a fact," and then he sticks his hand back in his apron pocket.

"Could I ask your name?" she says, kind of squinting at him.

"Joe," he says, like it's worse than getting a tooth pulled to give out his name.

"And who's this?" she asks, turning to me.

"That's my brother Roy," Joe says, only his voice is so quiet you can hardly hear him.

"You live here, Roy?"

"'Scuze me, ma'am," says Joe. "But what business is it of yours?"

The Indian lady, she gives him this real nice smile, and then she says, sweet as can be, "I'm the county truant officer, didn't you know? Now, why isn't Roy in school, can you tell me that?"

Joe Dilly don't say nothing at first, but he's got a look on his face that'll freeze water, and that truant officer, she hightails it back to her car.

Joe won't let it go. He follows her to the car and when she's inside with the windows rolled up and the door locked, he rears back and kicks the fender.

"Don't come back!" he yells, with his eyes like sparks of fire. "We won't be here!"

5

Joe Dilly Thinks It Over

I'm in the bunkhouse, packing up our gear, when Joe comes sloping in, and he throws himself down on his bunk and kicks his boots off and heaves them at the wall, thunk thunk.

"I done it now," he says. "I bet you're pretty disgusted with your big brother and his big mouth, am I right?"

"I never said that," I say.

Joe rolls over and folds his arms under his chin. "Don't need to say it," he says. "You know why we got to keep moving, don't you?"

"I guess."

"It ain't just what they'll do to me. They'll take you back there, Roy. You want to go back to that foster home?"

"I sure don't." Just thinking about it gives me a shiver.

"The law catches up to us they'll lock me up and throw away the key."

"We're all packed," I say. "Go on and get the truck."

Joe is jamming his feet back into his boots when Rick comes into the bunkhouse. He's got his hands in his pockets and you can tell he don't quite know how to say whatever it is he wants to say. Finally he spits it out.

"Hey, boys, what you up to?" he asks.

"Packing up."

"I can see that," he says. "You going someplace?"

"Joe Dilly don't like to hang around any one place for long," I say.

"That's how it is," Joe says. He's not looking at Rick, he's looking at his boots. "We got our reasons."

"I just now talked to Sally Red Dawn," Rick says. "The lady you run off."

"Don't matter," says Joe. "We're gone."

"Sally's a good lady," Rick says. "You ought to give her a chance, like she's willing to give you a chance."

Joe sits up straight. He's got this frozen look on his face. "What's that supposed to mean?"

"Means she'll mind her own business, for now. There's only two more weeks of school, then summer vacation, and Sally said she'd check back with you in September, make sure you sign up Roy for school."

"She said that?" Joe asks.

"I told her she caught you at a bad moment."

The way Joe looks at Rick, I'm afraid he's going to throw a punch or something, but then his face lights up and he tosses his head back and he laughs. "That she did!" he says. "We both had us a bad moment, and that's a fact."

"The point is," Rick says, "there's no reason to take off so quick. Stay for the summer. We got enough work to keep you both busy."

* * *

I keep my trap shut and wait for Joe to make up his mind. The truth is, me and Joe been a lot of places, but I never felt so lowdown about leaving before. Partly I'm mad at Joe, even if he can't help himself. This is all his fault, going crazy on that poor Sally Red Dawn when all she asked was a simple question. All I want him to do is give the Bar None a chance – maybe this time things can be different.

Joe, he's lying there on his back and staring up at

the bare wood of the ceiling and you can tell he's running stuff through his head, turning it over and thinking about it. Finally he says, "I guess you want to stay, huh?"

"Only if you do, Joe."

He sits up and looks me right in the eye. "Just the summer, Roy. Come fall, we'll be on our way."

I want to say something to him but I can't, it's like there's something inside my throat that won't let go, and so I just nod and start unpacking our gear.

When I turn around Joe Dilly ain't there. At first I think maybe he's took off without me, but then I spot him leaning against the corral fence, watching them Arabians showing off their high-stepping ways.

He's not doing nothing, just watching. You can tell he's worried about something, but I'm so happy we're staying I just let it go.

You can worry yourself to death, that's what Joe Dilly says, only he can't seem to take his own advice.

6
Rodeo Quality

Things go pretty good for a while. Rick don't mention Sally Red Dawn again, and Joe, it's like he never run her off.

You can tell when Joe Dilly's in a good mood, because he likes to whistle these stupid, boring old songs like "I'm Lookin' Over a Four-Leaf Clover". He'll keep that one going until it drives you crazy, except he looks so happy and contented you'll want him to whistle it for ever.

One day we're in the main barn. I'm doing my chores and mucking out the stalls and Joe is working to get a halter on Showdown and teach him some manners. He's whistling that "Four-Leaf Clover" song to beat the band when we hear this big truck come rumbling into the yard. Then this airhorn gives a blast that makes your knees rattle and Joe curses, because Showdown has shied away and now he won't have nothing to do with that halter.

I run outside to see what all the commotion is about, and there's this shiny tractor-trailer truck pulled up to the main corral, and the trailer is loaded up with horses. They're poking their heads out through the slats, trying to see what's going on, and you can see the nervous way their eyes roll and their nostrils twitch.

This tall guy with a long narrow face and squinty eyes gets down from the cab of that truck. He's wearing a faded denim jacket and pants tucked into his boots and a western shirt with fancy ivory buttons, and when he spots me he lifts his hat and gives me a little howdy-do nod. Underneath his hat his hair is flat white, but he don't really look that old. Even with his eyes all squinty you can see how blue they are, and how quick he is to look things over.

"There a horse ranch around here?" he says to me.

"You're on it," I say. "This is the Bar None, and there ain't no better horse ranch on the planet Earth."

The tall guy cracks a smile and says, "Is that a fact?"

"Yes, sir, it is."

Rick comes running out, and he takes one look at the long trailer chock full of horses and he throws his hat up in the air and gives a whoop, like it's Christmas morning and what he wants is right there under the tree.

"Son of a bee!" he shouted. "You did it!" and then all the other ranch hands come running and pretty soon there's a whole crowd of people gathered round, admiring that trailer full of horses.

Before long I figure out that the tall guy driving the truck is Mr. Nick Jessup, who owns the Bar None. Mr. Jessup has been travelling to auctions all over, to places like Arizona and New Mexico and Colorado, and he finally picked up all the horses he bought and brought them on home.

"We got mostly good solid Arabian broodmares, and just for the fun of it a real fine quarter horse," he tells everybody. "Rodeo quality."

Joe Dilly has come up behind me and he's standing there real quiet. Rick and the other hands, they set the ramp up so the horses can come down off the trailer, but Joe, he just keeps standing there, not saying nothing.

Finally Rick looks over and he says, "Hey Nick, there he is, the man I was telling you about."

Joe stirs but still he don't say nothing as Mr. Jessup

comes over and takes off his hat with one hand and holds his other hand out to shake. "I want to thank you for what you've done with Showdown," Mr. Jessup says. "That's mighty fine work. Rick told me all about it."

Joe takes his hand and shakes it real solemn. "It's nothing," he says.

Mr. Jessup, he grins and says, "All I know, it was a lucky day when you stopped by. Now who is this?" he asks, turning to me.

There's something about the way Mr. Jessup smiles that makes me like him right away. But Joe, he's acting tight and quiet like he does when he's afraid I'll talk too much, so I just tell Mr. Jessup my name and skedaddle back into the barn with Joe.

I keep hoping he'll whistle that "Four-Leaf Clover" song, but he stays quiet. It ain't just his voice – even his face is quiet. And when Joe Dilly gets all clenched up like that, the best thing is to shut up and keep working. So I do.

7
The Born Rider

The way it turns out, with all the chores needed doing in the main barn, I never get back to check out the new horses until lunch break. What I do is take my sandwiches and sit up on this broken old feed wagon, which is high up enough so you get a good view of the corrals.

Rick has got charge of the whole show, like you'd expect, and he's put the new horses in a holding area, near enough to some of the older horses so they can get acquainted, and sniff each other, but still kept far enough apart so they can't kick or tussle. Takes a while for horses to make friends with each other, just like with people.

Most of what Mr. Jessup brought in are Arabian broodmares, like he mentioned. That means they'll each have a baby horse once a year like clockwork, and the raising and selling of those foals is what keeps butter on the table at the Bar None – that's what Rick says.

I guess you already know how much I like them fine-looking Arabians, with their silky tails and pretty faces, but what has me curious is this new rodeo horse. They most always use quarter horses for rodeo work, and in case you don't know, they call it a quarter horse because it runs real fast for the first quarter mile. After that, your average Thoroughbred is a whole lot faster, which is why they end up breeding the quarter horse for working around the ranch. It has kind of short legs, but it's real powerful and sure-footed and quick, and you can train it to do most anything, which is why it makes the best rodeo horse. Rick says, you put the brakes on a quarter horse, you better hold on, because that animal can stop on a dime.

A real cowboy, working cattle and roping steer, I bet he won't have nothing but a quarter horse under him if he can help it.

Anyhow, Rick has put the new quarter horse in its own corral, and that horse is acting pretty calm and confident, considering he just got off a long ride in a trailer truck. His coat is this shimmery, golden brown that makes you want to run your hands over him, and the way he holds his head, it's like he knows he's important. I'm kind of edging my way along the corrals, because I don't want to spook him none, when suddenly there's this voice behind that makes me jump.

"That's Pit Stop," Mr. Jessup says. "He may be the best roping horse in this part of the world."

"He looks pretty near perfect," I say.

Mr. Jessup looks at me and then nods to himself. "You've got an eye for horseflesh, I can tell," he says. "You want to give me a hand with old Pit Stop?"

Joe Dilly probably wants me back in the barn, but I guess it'll be okay if I help Mr. Jessup instead. He puts this fancy roping saddle on Pit Stop and cinches it tight while I hold the halter and stroke his velvety brown throat, and I can tell right off that horse has got a peaceful and gentle disposition, and that he likes to be handled. Some horses, you try and slip the bit into their mouth, they'll kind of shudder and fight it, but Pit Stop is real polite. It's like he *wants* the bit in his mouth.

I'm just kind of standing there, watching Mr. Jessup ride that rodeo horse around the ring, when he turns to me and says, "Well, he's about warmed up. How'd you like to be the steer?"

At first I don't know what he's talking about. Then I see this rig set up on wheels, it don't look like a steer except it has a pair of fake horns up front.

What you do is push that contraption around the ring and Mr. Jessup throws his rope at it for practice.

He's pretty good, too. Mostly he gets his loop around the horns. Once he roped me, which gave us both a good laugh, and Pit Stop, well you never saw a horse move so smooth and certain. He never gets the least bit flustered or nervous, which is partly why he's a champion roping horse.

"I guess that's enough showing off for one day," Mr. Jessup says, coiling up his rope.

I figure he's done, and I'm getting ready to lead Pit Stop back to the corral and rub him down when Mr. Jessup stops me. "Hold on there," he says, and real quick shortens up the stirrups. He pats the saddle and says, "Go on, take him for a drive."

Of course there's nothing I want more than to try out a real rodeo horse, but for some reason my stomach feels like it's going down an elevator.

"You can't go wrong with this horse," Mr. Jessup says. "You make a mistake, he'll still do the right thing."

Well, I manage to get into the saddle without falling

off, which is a start, and Mr. Jessup hands me the reins and says, "Keep a soft hand."

That means don't yank on the reins.

"A horse trained like this one is, he's so used to going through his paces you don't hardly have to touch the reins at all," Mr. Jessup says. "You just shift your balance here and there, as natural as you can, and he'll know what you want."

That sounds too good to be true, but sure enough, Pit Stop is a mind reader. Before I'm hardly thinking "go left", he goes left, and there's something about the way he moves, it feels like you're just gliding along. Smooth and gentle and powerful all at the same time.

Mr. Jessup lets me run that fine roping horse around the ring for a while. I don't try nothing fancy, just getting a feel of how he moves, and I can tell Mr. Jessup thinks I'm doing okay. "Not bad for a little feller," he says. "Of course this animal is a size or three too big for you, but you manage to keep your balance in the saddle. You do a lot of riding, do you?"

"No, sir," I say. "I'm pretty busy helping Joe."

"Uh huh," he says, and he looks over my shoulder, like something has caught his attention.

That's when I notice Joe. He's standing in a shadow inside the barn and he's watching me. I don't know why, but it gives me this chilly feeling in my spine, like he's mad about something and I don't know what.

But then when I get back to the barn all he does is clap me on the shoulder, real friendly, and say, "I should have knowed you was a born rider."

8
One Fine Morning
Lady Luck Arrives

Pretty soon I'm out there every day helping Mr. Jessup.

In the morning he likes to work Pit Stop, what he calls a "tune-up" because he's got a funny way of talking about horses like they were cars or trucks. Like he'll say, "I'm gonna take this baby out for a spin," or "You drive for a while," or "Ask Joe can he check on the tyres," when he really means check the hooves.

Just because he talks like that, it don't mean he don't like horses, though. He's always real gentle in the way he handles them, and he hardly ever uses his spurs. He says, "A rider that keeps digging in his spurs is just plain ignorant."

Which makes me think I don't want a pair of spurs after all, even if they do look pretty cool the way they clip on your boots.

Then one fine morning I go to Pit Stop's stall and before I can clip on his lead rope, Mr. Jessup calls me out of the barn. "Leave that beast where he is for now!" he yells out. "Come on out here, Roy, I want to get your opinion on some horseflesh!"

So I go out to the yard and there's Mr. Jessup with the small trailer hitched up to his Ford pickup, and he's leading this little golden-coloured filly down the ramp. He's got hold of a soft rope halter and the filly is fighting him some – you can tell she's pretty scared. She's also the most beautiful creature you ever saw, so pretty she sort of glows from the inside.

"Roy, I'd like you to meet Lady Luck. She's almost three and just as green as she can be."

Before I know it, he's stuck that halter rope in my hand and it's all I can do to keep hold, the way she shies away from me. "Easy," I say, "easy there," but she's not in a mood to listen.

The filly has a fine, silky white mane and a tail like an Arabian, but she's small for a three-year-old, and Mr. Jessup says nobody knows for sure, she's probably part Arabian and part quarter horse, but she's small enough to be a pony.

"The little spitfire has been out to grass since she was born," he says. "Running wild. Never been broke or handled. You got your hands full, Roy – look how she prances!"

I can't hardly look because she's yanking me around so much. Mr. Jessup just stands back and watches – he's waiting to see what I'll do. Finally I get her settled enough so I can get up close and breathe into her nose, which is a trick Joe taught me, and what do you know, that gets her attention. She holds stock-still for just a moment, sniffing my breath. I work my hand up on the halter, where it wraps around her nose, and that filly, she starts to shiver and roll her eyes white, but she quits trying to pull on the halter rope.

"Lady," I say. "You sure are pretty, but you got to learn some manners."

Mr. Jessup is chuckling. "I think she likes you," he says.

Lady's looking me over with those big brown eyes of hers and I'm talking soft, not saying anything but just getting her used to the sound of my voice, and letting her smell me. There comes a moment when I can feel her change, right there in my hands. All those tensed-up muscles kind of relax and she decides to trust me.

"I'll be darned," Mr. Jessup says.

"You going to put a saddle on her?" I ask him.

47

"No," he says. "You are."

"Do you mean it?" I ask.

Mr. Jessup is looking us both over, me and Lady, and he nods his head to himself, like he's come to a decision. "If you can ride this pony, you can keep her," he says.

Then he starts to walk away, shaking his head. Before I can say anything he turns around and says, "More likely *she'll* keep *you*."

* * *

What happened is, I got so excited about Lady that I clean forgot about Joe. He's in the back stalls, working on an ornery stallion that split his back hooves, and I'm supposed to help him, soon as I'm finished with Mr. Jessup.

Well, Mr. Jessup goes off to tune up his rodeo horse, and I go into the small training ring with Lady Luck. I put this long lead on her halter, they call it a gyp rope, and just let her prance around the ring, feeling me there on the other end of the lead.

She's got a real springy step, like she don't hardly like to let her feet touch the ground, and she keeps rearing up and shaking her head, as if she wants me to know who's boss.

"Go on and run!" I tell her, circling around and paying out that rope to keep up with her. "Run till you fly!"

I swear, I almost expect that little horse to sprout wings, she's so light and airy on her feet. She keeps looking over at me and whinnying, like she's making conversation. Mostly she's saying, Look at me! Just look at me!

It's pretty cool, how you can feel a horse through the rope, as if the rope itself is alive, and it makes me so anxious to ride her I'm practically shaking inside. I feel like the anvil when Joe whacks it with his hammer, and it vibrates and hums. But you can't just throw a saddle on a wild horse or the horse will throw the saddle, or you, or even worse she might hurt herself. So you have to do it gradual, and let 'em get used to the idea.

That's what finally gets me thinking about Joe, because I want to ask him what should I do and how do I do it, and I want him to love Lady as much as I do already, and we barely been acquainted for an hour.

So I'm hanging on to that wild filly and thinking about Joe Dilly when suddenly I look over and he's standing there inside the barn, watching me. Man, it looks like his eyes are on fire, but that must be the sunlight or something.

Whatever it is, I accidently let go the gyp rope and Lady just plain goes nuts. She's running in about three directions at once, with the gyp rope whipping around, and before you can say jackrabbit that rope has caught up in her hind legs and she goes down and rolls over on her back with the rope all tangled everywhere and somehow wrapped around her neck. She's still going crazy, too, and she's got this wild look in her eyes like she can't breathe.

I'm just standing there like a total idiot, like a darn fence post stuck in the ground, and my heart is beating so hard I can't hardly see.

Next thing you know, Joe leaps over the fence rail and he's got his knife out, the wicked curved blade he cuts hooves with, and he leaps right on Lady where she's rolling and struggling on the ground. Somebody is screaming like a girl – me, as it turns out – and then the gyp rope comes loose and Lady quits struggling and lies there in the dirt, panting and getting her breath.

By the time I figure out how to move, Joe has her back up on her feet. She's wobbly but okay.

Joe, he's covered with sweat and dirt and a little blood from where he nicked his finger on the knife. He just looks at me and shakes his head.

"You're supposed to break a horse," he says, "not kill it."

9
What Joe Dilly
Sees in the Fire

Something gets into Joe Dilly after he saves that filly,
and he's so agitated he don't want to go into supper
with the rest of the hands.

"Mr. Jessup says he'd give you that pony? Now
why'd he do a thing like that, if he knows we're leaving
come the fall?"

Joe isn't talking to me, he's talking to himself the
way he does, scuffling around the bunkhouse and
running his fingers through his hair and looking like
something is about to jump out of a corner and go for
him, he's that spooked.

I'm sitting there on the edge of my bunk, staring at

the wood stove even though it ain't lit, just so's I won't look too close at Joe and get him more riled. Finally he pats me on the back and says, "Come on, Roy, whatcha waiting for, get your lazy backside up and let's go."

He's already at the screen door, waiting for me.

"Where we going, Joe?" He's got that look, like maybe he wants to hit the road and never come back.

"Just for a ride is all. You coming or what?"

I can't let Joe leave on his own, no matter how much I want to stay, so I get in that old pickup. Joe kicks it over and scoots out of the Bar None before I hardly get settled in the truck. Soon as the wheels hit the paved road he's feeling better. He's whistling and lighting up a cigarette and he's got that old Joe Dilly sparkle in his eyes. "What do you say, sports fans? You up for mystery meat surprise? I hear they got buffalo burger, and snake on a stick. You ever eat snake, Roy?"

I shake my head.

"They say it tastes like chicken, but they're lying. Snake tastes exactly like snake."

"Where we going, Joe?" I ask.

"You'll see," he says, acting like he's got a secret.

I'm thinking maybe I had it right about hitting the road, and I'll never see that pony again, when all of a sudden Joe pulls into this old gas station. There's a creaky lunch counter there, looks like something you see in an old magazine, but they have some hot dogs in the steamer, and we get a couple to go.

"Don't forget the mouse turd and the weepers," Joe says to the old guy behind the counter.

"What?"

"Mustard and onions," Joe says.

"I get it," the old man says, but he don't crack a smile.

Me, I just keep my mouth shut and go with a little ketchup.

We're almost out the door when Joe says, "Oops, I almost forgot," and he goes back in for a six-pack of beer.

I don't say nothing about the beer, but Joe notices how I'm looking at where it is on the seat between us. "Hell, Roy, there's nothing to worry about. Just a couple of beers is all. I been working hard, right? Ain't I been good? Couple beers never hurt a man on a Saturday night. Hell no."

I hate it when he drinks, but I don't say nothing and he turns on the radio and starts singing along with this crummy old song and looking at me sideways.

"I'm an old cowhand on the Rio Grande," he sings, making his voice go screechy-high and funny. "Just an old cowhand, on the Rio Grande." He keeps singing and making faces and sticking his tongue out at me until I can't help it, I'm laughing.

"That's more like it," he says. "Couple of good old boys in a pickup truck, that's how the West was won."

Another couple of miles down the road and he turns off onto this dirt trail, nothing but a couple of ruts overgrown with tall, spiky grass. He puts the truck in low gear and we bump along, and it's all I can do to keep my head from banging against the top of the cab. "Where we going, Joe?" I ask, spitting out the dust that's already mixed up with the hot dog.

"Top of the world!" he says. "Put on your oxygen mask, 'cause the air is getting thin!"

We go pretty high into those mountains, climbing along this switchback trail, until we come around the bend and there's a flat area that overlooks the whole valley. The sky is full of that thin blue twilight you get on a summer evening, and it hovers over everything, like maybe the sun will never get around to setting and the light will last for ever.

"Cool," I say.

"Cool? You mean you're cold?"

"You know what I mean," I say, and it really is cool, how you can see the Bar None from here, and the old gas station, and a bunch of other ranches, all laid out like on a chequerboard, except the Bar None has more squares than most of the other ranches.

"Take a deep breath," says Joe, getting out of the truck and stretching out his arms. "What do you smell?"

"Pine trees, I guess. And dirt."

"Okay, what *don't* you smell? I'll tell you what – you don't smell horses."

"I like the smell of horses."

"That's not the point," he says. He gets the beer out of the truck and sets it on the tailgate, so we can both sit and look over the valley. "The point is, this is another world up here. We could be anybody, sitting here. Anybody at all. Down there we're Horseshoe Joe and his little brother Roy. Up here, why, we could be princes. We could be kings!"

Joe has downed a couple of beers before you know it, and he's getting that look on his face that means he's changing inside. When he lights up a cigarette and cups his hand around the match, the fire is in his eyes again, like it was when he watched me from the barn. It's a scary look. I'm not afraid of Joe – he'd never hurt me, ever – but I'm scared of what he might do.

"You're shivering, Roy," Joe says.

"I'm okay."

He stands up and wipes his hands on his pants and says, "We got to warm ourselves up."

"I wish you wouldn't, Joe!"

He's already kicking some brush together. "Nothing

to worry about, sports fans," he says. "Just a small campfire. No law against a small campfire, is there?"

"You promised," I say. "You promised!"

Joe looks at me over the beer and he kind of freezes for a moment. "Listen here," he says. "What happened in Montana, that was an accident. It just got out of hand, is all."

"Let's go home," I say. "We don't need no campfire. Please?"

But it's like Joe won't listen to what he don't want to hear. He drinks the beer fast and then he stomps around and gathers up these old pieces of wood. Mostly tree branches and twigs and stuff. He kicks it all up together and before you know it he's crouching down and flicking his cigarette lighter. When that don't work he curses. "That darn wood is green," he says. "As green as that darn pony."

Then he opens the hood of the truck and squirts some gas from the carburettor into an empty beer bottle and he pours that on the wood and that does it, the fire takes off with a *woof!* that lifts his hat clean off his head.

When the flames are going good he sets back on the tailgate with me and it's like something has switched off inside him and he's the same old Joe again. "I didn't mean nothing about that pony, Roy.

She's a fine animal, and it's right you should want to keep her."

"We can leave anytime you want," I say.

Joe grips my arm. He's real intense, like something is bubbling inside him and wants to get out. "It's not what I want," he says. "I hope you understand that, Roy. It's what we have to do."

He gets up to tend the fire. You can feel the heat licking at us, it makes my face warm and my eyes hot, and the sparks rise up like lightning bugs, swirling and dancing in the air. It makes your head feel light, watching the sparks rise up.

The sun has finally gone down, and you can see the lights in the valley coming on, all them ranches lighting up. I'm seeing those ranch lights through the fire and it all blurs together and I feel like something really important is happening but I don't know what.

Beside me, Joe is working on his fifth bottle of beer. He don't ever get drunk, exactly, but it changes him into somebody else, somebody I don't know.

"You ever really looked inside a fire, Roy?" he says.

"I guess."

He's crouching by the fire now, poking at it with a stick, so close you think he'd get burned but he don't. "Look there, see how it comes alive? Them old church pictures show hell afire, but they've got it all wrong.

You're looking at heaven, Roy, all that light and heat and purity. There's angels inside that fire!"

I look but I don't see no angels. All I see is the heat and flames and how the fire makes Joe Dilly kind of crazy, how it fills him up inside until it has to come bursting out.

Then the smoke turns and my eyes start to water.

"You got no cause to worry this time," Joe says. "I promise you that."

"I ain't worried," I say.

But Joe knows I'm lying and he turns me towards him. I can smell the beer on his breath, and the onions. "Listen to me," he says. "That barn fire at the last place we worked, that was an accidental kind of thing. It won't happen again, you got my word on that."

I don't say nothing because the last thing I want to think about is what happened back in Montana, or what they say Joe done. Or how I seen him with that can of gas and the way his eyes looked crazy hot when that barn went up in flames. Because I know what Joe Dilly done and I know it wasn't no accident.

He drinks his last beer in one long gulp.

"Give a hand," he says, standing up. "Help me put this out."

We both of us kick dirt at the fire, but it don't die

down easy. The red heat of it keeps coming back through the dirt. Them branches look like hot bones glowing under the earth, and the way they twist and move it's like they're alive somehow. I get this idea that the flames are like blood, keeping the thing alive, but that don't make sense.

Joe thinks it's pretty funny, the way the fire won't go out, but I'm not laughing. I'm heaping clods of dirt at the glow and it keeps on breaking through and it's enough to make me cry, the way a fire keeps on burning, no matter what you throw at it.

"No!" I shout, and I'm stomping at them hot coals like a madman while Joe watches and shakes his head.

"And they say I'm crazy," he says.

On the third try we finally kill that fire, but even after it goes out I keep heaping dirt on it until Joe says, "That's enough," and he pulls me away.

"You think you can drive that truck?" Joe asks.

"My feet don't reach the pedals. You know that."

"I thought maybe that hot dog made you grow," Joe says. "I guess not."

"We could just sleep here," I say.

"No way," Joe says.

We get in the truck and he drives so slow I think we'll never get back to the Bar None. That ride just goes on for ever. So dark we could be inside a long, long tunnel, even though I know the sky is wide open, and there's nothing over us but black air. You can see the red eyes of the rabbits waiting alongside the road as the headlights go by, and I start counting the rabbits.

I must have fallen asleep somehow, because the next thing I know, Joe is setting me into my bunk and snugging up the covers, and I fall back to sleep thinking he smells just like the fire smelled when I tried to put it out.

10
Sacking the Sugar Beast

After that, Joe quit talking about how we'll have to leave come fall, and I just put it right out of my head I'm so busy with Lady Luck.

Mr. Jessup, when he's not messing with Pit Stop, he's helping me with Lady, and it's amazing how much he knows about training horses. You can tell from the very first time he comes into the barn, where Lady has a stall to herself, at least until the other animals get used to her.

"You ever break a pony, Roy?" he asks me.

"No, sir."

Mr. Jessup has a way of thinking for a while before

he talks. He'll shift his weight from one boot to the other and nod his head, until he's settled on what he wants to say. You have to be patient and not keep butting in or it takes for ever. Anyhow, he's rubbing his chin and squinting his eyes and finally he says, "There's a lot of ways to break a horse, but you boil it all down and it comes to this. You can either beat the animal into submission, or you can bribe it with sugar. Which way do you want to go with Lady?"

I don't have to think about that for even a second. "Sugar," I say.

"Good," says Mr. Jessup. He reaches into his shirt pocket and hands me a sugar cube. "Let's see if she's got a sweet tooth," he says. "Not every horse loves sugar right off the bat."

I hold the sugar cube in the palm of my hand and keep my hand flat so she can't accidently-on-purpose nip me. Lady takes a sniff of that sugar cube, but she don't open her mouth.

"She doesn't know what it tastes like," Mr. Jessup says. "You'll have to show her."

"You mean eat it myself?" I say.

Mr. Jessup laughs. "Nope," he says. "What you do is stick it in the corner of her mouth. Once she gets a taste, she'll want more."

Sure enough, when I slip that sugar cube into the

side of her mouth, she chews it up and shakes her head and snorts. "I think she likes it," I say.

"That's enough for now," Mr. Jessup says. "Let her get used to one idea at a time. You brush her good, and after you finish, see if she'll take a cube from your hand."

So I give her a good brushing. You have to go with the grain and not fight the way her coat grows, and if you do that, you can tell she likes the feel of that brush stroking her skin. When her coat is clean and shiny and glowing I set to work on her mane. It's her Arabian blood that makes her mane so long and fine and silky so the comb just glides through real smooth. She gets a little frisky when I comb out her tail, though, like she wants to turn around and see what I'm doing back there.

"You want some more sugar, is that it?" I say. "You'll have to learn some patience."

Another thing you have to get a horse used to is lifting its feet. Joe showed me the trick of getting a hoof up, where you lean your weight against the leg and reach down and touch behind the knee with one hand while you lift the foot with the other. Pretty soon that horse will learn to lift up its feet just by touch, and you can use a pick to keep the bottom of the hoof clean, where it gets caked with dirt and manure. You don't do that and a horse with dirty hooves will come down with thrush, which is a bad infection that will make it go lame.

Anyhow, I try that trick on Lady, touching behind her knee, and what do you know, she fights me! She stands there with her weight balanced and just plain refuses to pick up her feet, no matter how much I nudge her.

Finally, I lose my patience. I look her in the eye and say, "Pick up that foot or else!"

She tries to rub her head against me, looking for sugar, but I won't have none of that. "I ain't leaving until you learn to pick up your foot," I say. "That's the long and short of it."

The next time I try, she snorts and sighs and then finally lifts her foot, as if to say, oh big deal, take a look if you want, it's all the same to me.

You're probably thinking she'll get the sugar for lifting her foot, right? Wrong. I do that, she'll want a lump of sugar for every hoof, and once you start a horse in on a bad habit, they keep it up – I know that much from listening to Joe. So I wait until she's forgotten about her feet and when I hold out my hand, she carefully sniffs the cube and then *slurp!* she's chomping away on it and making contented noises that mean she's happy.

Which makes me happy, too.

* * *

The next morning when Mr. Jessup comes into the barn he's carrying an empty feed sack. "This is an old trick," he says, handing me the sack. "Maybe it'll work and maybe it won't."

I'm standing there holding the empty sack like a goon, because I don't know what to do with it. Mr. Jessup finally notices and he says, "Oh, right. The sack. Okay, what are we trying to do with this pony?"

"Get a saddle on her," I say.

He nods. "Exactly. She has to get used to the feeling of something on her back. Start with the empty sack. Go on, just drape it over her back, like it was a saddle."

Of course it ain't a saddle, but I do like he says. Lady, she sort of shivers and that sack comes floating down off her back.

"Keep trying," Mr. Jessup says. "Rub her legs with it and flick it around until it doesn't spook her any more. When she leaves it on, give her a lump of sugar. That's the bribe. You're teaching her good behaviour. Just keep that in mind, you'll be okay."

He hands me this bag of sugar cubes and I hide it outside the stall, so Lady can't sniff it out and cause a fuss. First thing I do, like Mr. Jessup suggested, is I get Lady used to the idea of something going on around her back and legs. I keep laying that sack on her and pulling it off and kind of flicking it against her withers.

Well, she makes a game of it, twitching her tail and tossing her head, but finally she gets tired or maybe bored and she quits snorting and shaking her head and she ignores that fluttering sack – it don't bother her no more than a fly.

After that, I leave her alone for a while. The way a horse thinks, it needs time to settle in.

So I go on and give Joe a hand, where he's working this purebred Arabian mare that's picked up a bad habit of kicking. He's got her in cross-ties so she can't move around too much, and he's checking her out, real cautious. "It ain't a mean streak that makes her kick," he says. "Somebody hurt her once, before she came to the Bar None. Mr. Jessup knew, and he took her anyway."

"Will she try and kick you, Joe?" I ask.

"Don't matter who," he says. "The habit of kicking has dug deep into her mind."

"Can you stop her?"

Joe shrugs. "I'll give her a good try," he says.

When Joe hears about Mr. Jessup's idea of sacking Lady to get her used to a saddle, he don't say much, he only nods.

"If you got a better way, you only got to tell me," I say.

"You go on like he told you," Joe says. "Sack the sugar beast. That's as good a way as any."

"You mean it?"

"'Course I do," he says, and that's an end to it.

After lunch, which I didn't eat much, I go back and try that sack again. Because maybe she's forgot by now, and I'll have to start over. But when I slip the sack over her back, right where the saddle will go, she don't even try to shake it off! She just looks me over, like she's saying: What do you think I am, stupid?

I run back outside to the riding ring to tell Mr. Jessup the good news. He don't act the least bit surprised. Rick is helping him put Pit Stop through his paces, cutting tight around these barrels they've set up in the ring, and Mr. Jessup turns to Rick and says, "What do we have in the way of small saddles?"

Rick looks at me and grins and says, "Come with me."

The tack room at the Bar None is bigger than on most ranches because Mr. Jessup, he don't like to throw nothing away. That's what Rick says. First thing, you go into the tack room, you can smell the leather and oil, which is a good smell. There's all these pegs on one wall, with bridles and halters hanging there. Mr. Jessup has a whole other wall reserved for his ropes and lariats, because they have to be just right. Then there's like this long set of rails where they keep the saddles, and there's every kind of saddle. There's this one cowboy saddle that looks so old you're almost afraid to touch it, and Mr. Jessup says it was owned by an outlaw called John Wesley Hardin.

"Old John Wesley Hardin probably stole that saddle from a hard-working cowboy, but I paid good money for it at auction," Mr. Jessup says. "You look over there on the left side, there's a bullet hole."

I look, and sure enough, there *is* a bullet hole.

"Had the horse he stole shot out from under him," Mr. Jessup says. "Which is a sin, shooting an innocent horse."

"What happened to John Wesley Hardin?" I ask.

"He was on the run for a long time," Mr. Jessup says. "But in the end the law finally caught up to him. Like it usually does."

Rick hears that and he clears his throat and says, "About that saddle," like he wants to change the subject. So Rick pulls out a few saddles, one by one, and Mr. Jessup looks them over and finally nods at a small one and says, "That'll do. You carry it, Roy, see can you heft it."

There's some saddles I can't even pick up, they're so heavy, but this one is pretty light, although it does seem to get heavier and heavier the longer you carry it.

Anyhow, we get that saddle back to the holding pen, with me carrying it all the way by myself, and

Mr. Jessup says, "You tired, son? We can wait until tomorrow, the pony won't mind."

I'll mind, though, so I take a deep breath and say, "I'll get this saddle on Lady if it kills me."

Rick laughs and says he hopes it don't come to that.

I figure they'll let me do it on my own, and they do, except everybody wants to watch. When I bring Lady out from her stall to the holding pen, Rick and Mr. Jessup are there, leaning on the fence rail. Even Joe comes out from where he's been working with the kicker, and he hangs up his leather apron and folds his arms and says, "You get a saddle on that pony and I'll eat spinach for supper." He hates spinach worse than anything.

"You better work up an appetite," I say.

But when I get into the pen with her, Lady rolls her eyes, like she's thinking, *You better not try anything fancy on me, boy.* But she don't fight when I clip her halter to the post. Maybe she's waiting to see what happens next.

The truth of it is, I don't know what happens next. It's like Rick and Mr. Jessup and Joe are waiting for me to figure it out on my own.

I'm about ready to get it over with and just heave that little saddle up on her quick when I get this idea.

First I take that old sack and shuck handfuls of grain in until it weighs as much as the saddle, near as I can tell. Then I slip the weighted sack up on Lady and she dances around some, but she don't shake it off.

I look over then and see Rick and Mr. Jessup and Joe, and they're all watching me. One by one they nod to let me know filling the sack was the right idea.

"Can't I have a little privacy?" I ask.

So they all turn their backs and pretend they're not looking but they are.

"Fine," I say. "See if I care."

I get the saddle balanced on the fence rail where I can reach it, and I loop one stirrup up over the horn so it don't get in the way. Then I stroke Lady for a while, until she's calm and not moving around much. Next thing, I slip the grain sack off her back, and before she hardly knows it's gone, I replace it with a light saddle pad. Then I grab hold of that saddle and slip it up on her back, over the pad. She makes a little snort, like What's this? But before she can figure it out, I reach up under her belly and grab the cinch strap and slip it into the rings.

After I get the cinch snugged up, I give Lady her sugar. That's all I figure to do, get that saddle on her, but she seems so gentle and relaxed I decide why not get it over with? Why not go the whole way to the moon?

So without really thinking about it, I put my foot in the stirrup and grab hold of her neck and swing myself up into that saddle. Once I get there, Lady kind of dances sideways, pulling against the halter rope, and I have to grab hold of the saddle horn and hold on for dear life, but she don't really try to buck me off. Before you know it she settles down and just stands there, flicking her tail, like it was the most natural thing in the world, having a boy on her back.

"Good girl," I say, and lean down to stroke her neck and give her a lump of sugar.

Then it hits me, what I just did, and I start feeling kind of shaky. I don't know what got into me, to get up on her back so soon, and I been so concentrated I clean forgot about the audience until Joe lets out a whoop.

"You see that?" he says, slapping his hat against his leg. "You see that runt of a boy tame that wild pony in a day? What do you think of that, sports fans!"

Then he starts slapping high fives all around and Mr. Jessup and Rick are shaking their heads and grinning. "Oh, I suspected he might have the gift," Mr Jessup says. "He got it from you, Joe."

"Never mind where he got it," Joe says. He's practically jumping up and down, he's that excited. "Where's the spinach? I'm so hungry I could eat it raw!"

That's the funniest thing, how happy Joe is when I get a saddle on Lady Luck. I figured he didn't like the idea of that pony, or the way Mr. Jessup promised her to me, but Joe Dilly, he'll surprise you sometimes.

11
What the Grizzly Bear Said After I Fell Asleep

As it turns out, getting the saddle on Lady was the easy part. Because the next day when I try to put the bit in her mouth, she clamps up her teeth and won't have nothing to do with it.

When I can't get her to take the bit, not even with lumps of sugar shoved in first, Mr. Jessup gives it a try. He holds the loop up against her head like you're supposed to, ready to slip it over her ears. Then he pries at the hard part of her jaws, and tries to slide the rubber bit between her teeth, but Lady fights him, too. She just won't have none of it.

Mr. Jessup stands back and looks her over. "We

could keep fussing with her," he says. "Eventually she'll have to give up. Or we could switch gears and go with a hackamore rig for now."

A hackamore is like a soft rope halter. Instead of putting a bit behind the horse's teeth, it tightens up around the nose and mouth. Some trainers like to use it from the start, so the inside of the horse's mouth won't get hard from the bit. Anyhow, we go with a hackamore and Lady don't like it much, but she don't fight us real hard as we slip it over her nose.

"There," says Mr. Jessup. You can see where the beads of sweat have collected along his upper lip, which seems to happen when he concentrates real hard. "Don't be afraid to be firm," he says to me. "She has to learn that you're the boss."

Which is easier said than done, as it turns out. She lets me get up in the saddle okay, but the first time I pull on the reins she fights me and skitters sideways, bumping up against the rail. It's all I can do to keep from falling off.

"Drop the reins," Mr. Jessup says. "See what she does."

The last thing I want to do is drop those reins, because what if she gets it into her mind to buck me off? Cowboys, they don't think anything of it, getting thrown, but there's nothing about falling off that I like.

Still, I do what Mr. Jessup wants and let the reins drop, and what happens is exactly nothing.

Lady just stands there. Then she lowers her head and sniffs at the reins. When she's satisfied she lifts her head and looks at me, as if to say, Oh, is that all? What was I making such a fuss about?

"Pick 'em up slow," Mr. Jessup says. "That's it. Now instead of pulling back, lay the reins against the side of her neck and give her a little nudge with your heels. And remember to shift your weight back in the saddle."

When I give her a nudge, Mr. Jessup taps behind her back feet with his long, stiff-handled whip. Of course he don't whip her with it, he just taps, so she'll start to go forward, which she does. I lay them reins against her neck and she turns the opposite way, with a little encouragement from Mr. Jessup, and before you know it, she's walking around the ring.

"Ha!" cries Mr. Jessup, and he snaps the whip in the air.

Lady hears that, and all of a sudden she's trotting, keeping her feet high to get away from where the whip is tickling her ankles. I'm taken by surprise almost as much as she is, but I manage to stay in the middle of the saddle and keep hold of her with my knees, like you're supposed to, and try not to look scared, even though I am, a little bit.

"Stop her now!" Mr. Jessup yells out, and I almost forget what I'm supposed to do, until it comes to me. You have to squeeze with your legs and pull back on the reins and shout "Ho!"

I have to do it three or four times before she figures out what I want, with a little help from Mr. Jessup.

"That's enough for today," he says, putting away his training whips. "You go on and help Joe. Tomorrow we'll take her out on the trail, see how she behaves when she's outside a corral."

"You mean it?"

He shrugs. "Why not?"

I go right into the stable and tell Joe and he says, "That's nice," and then he hands me the shovel and the broom. "Go ahead, Hercules. You put the hay in one end, now clean up after the other."

I'm in such a fine mood it don't matter how many stalls got to be mucked out, because all I can think about is taking Lady out on the trail. In real life I'm inside the barn, shovelling up about a million tons of fresh manure, but inside my head I'm gliding over the meadows on Lady, and we're running so fast that we don't weigh more than a feather or two, and the amazing thing is how smooth and graceful it seems, like we don't touch the ground at all. Like I'm part of the horse, or she's part of me.

Of course, this is all daydream kind of stuff. Except it feels so real. It makes me happy but I figure it won't last long. You can't hold on to a thing like that.

* * *

Later on, after I finish up my chores and we chow down, me and Joe sit around the bunkhouse. He's perched up in this old ratty leather armchair he favours, smoking one cigarette after another, like something is on his nerves. Times like this I just keep quiet, so I don't set him off. You don't fool with Joe Dilly when he's got something on his mind.

After a while he says, "They do give me slack, here at the Bar None, you got to give 'em that much. That's all I ever want, just let me do things my own way."

"They like you, Joe," I say.

"Ain't being liked I'm talking about," he says. "It's being left alone to do the job the best way you see fit. Mostly, as you know, I don't think much of the bosses and owners, but Rick and Mr. Jessup, they're okay in my book. So far."

That's a change of pace, Joe saying he don't mind the boss, and I take it as a good sign. Maybe that fire I saw in his eyes was just the sun catching him, and he really is over and done with getting in trouble, like he promised. Except for that time up on the mountain, he's been real calm since we come to the Bar None, and he don't seem ready to fight at the drop of a hat, like he used to.

I'm lying sideways on my bunk, counting the knotholes in the pine boards but not keeping track, kind of waiting to see what he'll say next. Even though part of me is on edge, it's real peaceful. I like hanging out in the bunkhouse, just me and Joe, with the air so still outside you can hear the horses snorting and snuffling, and the soft click of their hooves on the hard floor, and the silvery sound of cool water trickling into the troughs. Somewhere off in the distance there's an owl hooting, and it gives me a nice little shiver – I don't know why, but that wild bird sound always makes me feel lonesome in the best way.

After a long while, Joe gets real calm and puts away his cigarettes and says, "You better turn in, Roy. You're going riding with the boss, you'll want a clear head."

"What if she bucks me, Joe?"

He looks at me and nods kind of slow. "I don't think she will, from what I seen of her. But if she does buck, you just hang on and try to turn her if you can. That's all you can do. Sooner or later every horse stops."

"Maybe you could come with us," I say. I been

waiting all day to ask him and this is the first chance I had, when his mood seems okay.

But Joe shakes his head real firm. "I ain't been invited. Besides, I got more than I can handle such as it is, without taking a day off to tour the back country."

"But you don't mind if I do?"

"Why should I mind?" he says. "It ain't right a boy your age should have to work like a full-growed man. You go on and have a good time for once."

Sooner or later I fall asleep and I'm pretty sure there's a grizzly bear in my dreams. This big old quiet bear sits up almost like a man on his haunches and he's watching as me and Lady canter by, and he raises his paw as if to say, "You haven't got a worry in the world. Nothing can catch you, not even me."

It don't scare me, that dream about the bear. Matter of fact, I kind of like it.

12
We're in High Cactus Now

You get the impression, coming over the ridge, that the Bar None goes on for ever, but when I ask Mr. Jessup how big the ranch is, he says, "Big enough," and leaves it at that.

We been out on the trail for a mile or more before the sun comes up and turns everything the colour of pink cotton candy, the kind will make your teeth hurt with sweetness. Mr. Jessup stops his rodeo horse and takes a deep breath, like he wants to inhale that pretty pink colour, which before long starts to turn into that shade of orange you get when you crack open a fresh cantaloupe.

Maybe I'm thinking about candy and melons because we ain't had breakfast yet. The way it works, you have to get up early in the morning if you want to ride the back country at the Bar None. I figure Lady was so easy to saddle because she was still asleep, and here she is following along behind Pit Stop and Marzy Doats like it's the most natural thing in the world. You already heard about Pit Stop, and Rick's horse is called Marzy Doats, from some dumb old song I never heard before. He's this old, toffee-coloured gelding with a star blaze on his forehead and white stockings, and Rick says he's a real gentleman with manners better than most people.

After Mr. Jessup gets a sniff of the sunrise, he giddyaps his horse and says, "Let's get a move on, I smell coffee."

I take a deep breath, but all I smell is green grass and morning dew and a couple of fresh horse buns old Marzy Doats left steaming on a rock. But pretty soon I figure out that's just the way Mr. Jessup talks about things, because what he means about smelling the coffee is that it's time to make some. There's this spot further on down the trail, just where it starts to level out at the bottom of the valley, where stones have been laid out in a circle, and you can see the black and soot from a lot of campfires.

We stop there and tie off the horses while Rick unpacks all this cooking gear from his saddlebags.

"I bet you worked up an appetite," Mr. Jessup says. "What'd we bring for grub? Hardtack and beans?"

"Cold beans," says Rick. "And mouldy biscuits."

You'd never know they're fooling to hear them talk, but they are, because before you know it, Rick is brewing up a pot of boiled coffee over an open fire and he's got a big iron skillet spattering with slabs of bacon and fresh eggs and brown bread from a can. Rick puts evaporated milk in his tin mug of coffee, but I take mine black just like Mr. Jessup, and I like it fine.

Nothing ever smelled so good as that thick bacon sizzling away, and like Mr. Jessup says, we're about ready to chew the saddles off the horses before Rick heaps it all in these dented tin plates he carries around in his saddlebags. "What you do is mush up the eggs on the brown bread and pick your teeth with the bacon," he says. "Go on and try it."

He don't have to tell me twice. We set ourselves down around the campfire and just dive into that food and I'm wishing Joe Dilly would have come along, because he sure would get a kick out of this. How clear and right and simple everything seems when you're outside under a big sky, and you're hungry, and there's plenty of good food to eat.

"You notice how sure-footed that pony was, coming down the steep part of the trail?" Rick says to Mr. Jessup.

Mr. Jessup sips his coffee and nods. "I noticed," he says.

"You can't teach an animal to be sure-footed," Rick says to me. "They have it or they don't."

"Lady's the best pony in the world," I say.

Rick and Mr. Jessup look at each other and smile. Rick says, "I remember my first horse, Serita. She was a broodmare that couldn't foal no more, so she wasn't worth but a few dollars. I sure did love her though."

"Mine was Bart," Mr. Jessup says. "A mustang stallion. I never did break him. He broke me."

"More coffee?" asks Rick.

"Don't mind if I do," says Mr. Jessup.

"Fill 'er up," I say, holding out my mug, too, and for some reason that makes them both laugh. They give me the coffee, though, and another helping of bacon, and by the time we climb back up on the horses I'm about ready to burst.

We go along slow until the food shakes out and settles, like Rick says, and all I have to do is keep my balance and look around to see Lady don't step in a gopher hole. She sees 'em before I do, though, and picks her way around.

Mr. Jessup rides on ahead a little ways, and that's when I notice he's got his own personal way of riding. He sits up real straight in the saddle and his feet kind of pedal in the stirrups, like he's walking. I try to do it, but it won't work for me, so I go back to my own way.

It's just starting to really warm up so you can see the heat making the ground blurry when Mr. Jessup points up to a bluff and says, "If you don't mind, I'm going to pay my respects."

Rick stops his horse while Mr. Jessup rides on up to the bluff on his own. When he's most of the way up there Rick says to me, "That's where he and Sadie and little Nick used to picnic."

When I don't say nothing, Rick takes off his hat and goes, "I guess maybe you didn't know that Mr. Jessup had a wife and child that died. Road accident. Hit by a drunk cowboy."

I don't know what to say about that, because it seems so awful. But maybe that's why Mr. Jessup sometimes looks like he's listening real hard when there's nothing to hear.

"Little Nick would be about your age now," Rick says. "Don't mention I told you unless he brings it up himself."

"I won't," I say.

The funny thing is, when Mr. Jessup comes back

down from the bluff he don't look sad at all. He looks exactly the same, except he's even more quiet than usual.

"Lovely morning," he says. "Let's ride on."

So that's what we do, we ride on, away from the ridge and the bluffs and the steep parts of the trail, and all around us the country starts to change, real gradual. Where before it was all wild grass and rolling fields of alfalfa, and here and there stands of low piney trees, now you can't find but a few blades of grass. There's mostly just rusty-looking dirt and a few straggly cactus, and once in a while an old mesquite tree so thick with knuckles and twigs it looks like somebody throwed it away.

Rick calls this place the back country, and he says it's pretty close to the high desert except not quite so dry. It ain't lush or green, but there's something about it I like. The way you can see where the wind blows by the way it squiggles up the dirt in long furrows, and the quiet in your ears, and the feeling of how big the sky gets, and how far away it looks to the edge of the world.

I guess some folks think all that emptiness looks plain ugly, but I feel right at home even though I've never been to this spot before. It just seems right, like I already know this place in my bones and under my skin.

"We're in the high cactus now," Rick says. "Once in a blue moon it rains out here. Then all the flowers bloom."

I figure they're pulling my leg except nobody laughs, so I guess it really does happen sometimes, even if you can't see anything like a flower in all that red dirt.

Lady seems to like it, too. She keeps snorting and checking out the high desert smells, and sometimes she skitters sideways if a gust of wind licks her. I keep the reins in my left hand like you're supposed to, but it don't really matter about the reins because Lady just follows along behind Rick's horse, and walks where he walks. She knows more about it than I do.

We must have come a couple or three miles into the back country, following this trail that looks like it might have been a creek bed once upon a time, when all of a sudden Lady stops dead in her tracks. She puts her head up and flicks her ears forward and makes this whinny sound deep in her throat.

I'm about ready to give her a giddyap and put her mind back on her business when suddenly I hear this dry, ratchety noise, sounds like somebody winding on a broken music box.

"Rattlesnake," says Rick.

That's the last thing he says to me for a while

because right about then Lady takes off like a bolt of lightning.

It happens so fast I can't tell how it started. One second she's standing there, sort of frozen and scared, and the next she's going about a hundred miles an hour, straight at this patch of sorrel cactus, and I'm hanging on for dear life.

The only reason I don't fall off and break my neck is I'm too surprised to think. There's nothing in my head but this bright yellow noise, and it's all I can do to wrap my arms around her neck and hold on tight. The reins are flying over my head and there's no way Lady can miss this bunch of cactus that are coming up faster than a rocket. I figure I'll look like a pincushion, or worse.

Then suddenly she leans to the other side, dodging around, and the cactus are flying by so close I can feel the wind they make, and she's turning so hard and fast the red dirt is exploding under her hooves like hand grenades or something.

For a second I get a look behind me and there's Mr. Jessup riding hell-bent for leather, trying to catch up. He's smacking his hat on Pit Stop's rump, and that rodeo horse is flat out, but he's not gaining much.

Then I can't look back because Lady is scrabbling sideways to get around another cactus, and the way she lunges ahead, stretching her neck out and picking up speed, it makes me think she's got over being scared and now she's having fun.

I ain't having much fun, though. Bent over like I am with my arms around her neck, that saddle horn is banging right into my gut, and finally I just give up and sit back and expect the worst.

I figure the only reason I don't fall off is I worked up such a sweat that I'm stuck on that saddle like a suction cup. Right about then the reins bounce up near to hand and I try pulling back, not that Lady's in a mind to pay attention – she's having a wild time of it going fast and seeing if she can run backwards and upside-down all at the same time.

What happens in the end is she tires herself out and finally slows down and puts on the brakes on her own, without any help from me. She's standing there shaking her head and sneezing on all the dust she raised, and that's when Mr. Jessup catches up.

Both he and his horse look the same rusty colour, all lathered up with the dirt and dust, and his eyes are squinted almost shut. I can tell he's looking at me, though. He shakes his head and coughs and after he gets his breath back he says, "Holy cow, that was a run, wasn't it? How'd you manage to stay on, if you don't mind me asking?"

I tell him my theory about the sweat making my butt into a suction cup and he gets to laughing so hard he starts to cough again. Then Rick catches up to us on old Marzy Doats, and he gets down and rummages around in his saddlebag and gives us each a rag to clean up with, and he passes around a water canteen, which really hits the spot.

"What do you think?" Rick says to Mr. Jessup. "Aside from the fact that this boy is a natural-born rider, I mean."

Mr. Jessup takes a swig out of the canteen and screws the lid back on, real careful. "I think I never saw a pony so fast out of the gate," he says. "And did you see the way she cut around that sorrel cactus and then took off?"

"I saw it," says Rick.

"You thinking what I'm thinking?" says Mr. Jessup.

"I expect so," says Rick.

"Yep," says Mr. Jessup, nodding to himself. "This little filly might have the makings of a quarter-mile racer."

Soon as he says that I get this sick feeling inside, because I figure that means he'll want her back. So at first it don't sink in when he says, "What do you think, Roy? You want to race your pony in the rodeo?"

13
Just Say Geronimo

I find Joe Dilly in a stall with Showdown, fussing at him, and the big stallion don't move so much as an eyelid while Joe licks his hooves with that rasp file. As much time as Joe seems to spend with the horse, which nobody else can touch, he don't show no interest in riding him. Like it's enough to just handle his feet and make him comfortable.

"You look like you been up to no good," he says, right off the bat. "Am I right?"

"Not exactly," I say. "Except I almost died, and it sure was fun."

So I tell Joe about the back country and the

rattlesnake and the way Lady took off quick as lightning, and how she finally stopped on her own.

"You stuck on that saddle like glue, did you?" he says. "I might have known."

"You're the one taught me how to keep my balance," I say.

"Ah, you had it from the get go." He lights up a cigarette and coughs a little and says, "Is this pony really as fast as they think she is?"

I shrug and go, "I'm still kind of blurred from it all," which gets a laugh out of Joe Dilly. "You're a lucky kid, you know that, Roy? Situation could be a whole lot worse, you think about it."

He means that crummy foster home, before he came in like a storm and sprung me free, and as soon as he says that, it kind of crashes together inside me, that maybe we shouldn't be here at the Bar None at all, not with Sally Red Dawn sniffing around and getting official come the fall. The law finds out about how Joe sprung me without bothering to get legal custody, or that stuff in Montana, and we'll both of us end up in bad places.

"Hey, don't worry," Joe says. "You gotta take this life one day at a time. You got the whole summer ahead of you, right?"

"You mean it?" I ask.

"Sure I do," he says.

But a while later I catch him when he don't know I'm looking, and he's got his forehead all wrinkled up and you can see he's worried, and all that happy talk about the summer was just to make me feel good.

* * *

I put it out of my mind, though, when Mr. Jessup comes into the stables the next morning and asks how do I feel about putting Lady up against the clock?

He wants to know how fast she runs, and when I saddle her up and bring her out, he and Rick have measured the distance they want her to run. They got a sawhorse for a starting gate and another one set up for the finish.

Lady looks it over and gets a little nervous. I know because she's prancing and pulling on the halter. "Easy there, girl," I say. "Those ain't rattlesnakes, they're just old sawhorses is all."

"You ever seen a quarter-mile race, Roy?" Mr. Jessup wants to know.

"No, sir," I say. "Joe took me to a rodeo once, but I was too small to see over the side. I could hear all the people cheering, though, and see the hats flying by."

Mr. Jessup crouches down and starts drawing lines in the dirt with a little stick. "It's pretty simple. The bell goes off, the gate opens, and you get your horse to the end of the track as fast as you know how."

Rick has got a stopwatch hanging on a string around his neck. He says, "A Thoroughbred wouldn't know how to run as short a distance as four hundred and forty yards, which is the same as a quarter mile. That's where a smaller horse has the advantage, if it gets up to top speed clean off the start. Is that about right, Nick?"

"Yes, sir, it is," says Mr. Jessup. "You ready to give it a go, Roy?"

"I'm ready," I say, hoisting myself up into the saddle and picking up the reins. "What do I do?"

Mr. Jessup squints into the sun until all I can see is blue slits looking at me. "Try not to slow her down too much," he says. "Try not to fall off."

Well, you never really know what a horse is going to do before it does it, and Lady don't seem to be in the mood to run. I get her back behind the first sawhorse and give her a giddyap nudge with my heels, but all she does is amble along like she's in the mood for a long slow walk.

Rick looks up from his stopwatch and when he sees Lady taking her own sweet time, he kind of grins and shakes his head.

Mr. Jessup, he don't wait around, he heads into the barn without looking back.

I'm going, "Come on, Lady! Go! Go!" but don't you know, that pony acts like she can't hear me, and she's wandering around sniffing at the sawhorses and generally making herself at home. I might as well not even be there, as far as she's concerned.

"Lady, please? Don't you want to be a racehorse?"

Nothing.

I feel like such a fool I'm about to start bawling like a baby when Mr. Jessup comes back out of the stable holding something shiny in his hands. I can't tell what he's thinking from the look on his face. Could be he's laughing at me, or he might even be angry, you never know with him.

But when he gets a little closer I see what he's holding. A small pair of spurs.

"Wasn't sure if we had anything your size," he says. "But I found these in an old milk crate. I do believe these were my first pair of spurs."

They're the kind of spurs clip right on the heel of your boots. Mr. Jessup sticks them on for me and then he pats me on the knee and says, "You know the trick with spurs, do you?"

"No, sir, I don't."

"The trick is you don't use 'em much. And you don't dig them in and hurt the horse, like you see those cowboys do on TV. All you want to do, give this pony a signal she can't ignore. That rattlesnake surprised her, and so she took off, but the thing of it is, after she got running she ran because she loved it. Some animals will get intoxicated with speed, and they make the best racers. So once you get her moving, I'm pretty sure she'll go fast because she wants to."

"What do I do?" I ask.

"Get her behind the line again and stop her. I mean hold on the reins and tense up, so she knows something is about to happen. Then all at once you relax your legs, nudge your heels into her side, slap the reins, and yell 'Geronimo!'"

"You mean it?"

"Yell anything you like, just so you make a lot of noise."

I get her back behind the starting line okay, and she starts to fight me when I pull back on the reins.

"Good, good!" says Mr. Jessup. "That'll make her want to go."

He says "tense up" and that part is easy, since I already feel like a watch that got wound too tight. Anyhow, I hold her back and count three to myself and then I kick with the spurs and slap her with the reins and shout "Geronimo!" at the top of my lungs.

Next thing I know, Lady has took off like a scalded

cat, only she's not heading for the finish line like she's supposed to. She's headed off down the trail, like she thinks we're going for the back country.

She's moving so fast I can't think quick enough to keep up, and it's all I can do to hold on.

I get her steered back, but Lady never does cross the finish line. She's too busy spooking herself with those sawhorses. She acts like they're alive, like she wants to charge right at them and scare them off.

When I finally get her stopped she's all lathered up and shiny with sweat and she's pitching her head around and looking back at me as if to say, What do you think of that, sports fans?

Rick and Mr. Jessup come over and Rick is looking at his stopwatch and shaking his head. "What do you make of it?" he asks.

Mr. Jessup look at the watch and shrugs. "I'm not exactly sure," he says. "Of course if this had been a race, she'd have been disqualified for leaving the track."

Rick goes, "Heck, Nick, you saw the clock, she's a natural."

"Maybe," says Mr. Jessup. "She's fast, I'll grant you that." Then he looks at me and says, "Well, did you like it?"

"We'll go faster next time," I say.

Rick and Mr. Jessup look at each other and Mr.

Jessup smiles and says, "That's what I wanted to hear. You feel good?"

"Yes, sir, I do."

It's the truth. I feel good about everything. Lady and Joe Dilly and summer at the Bar None. But the thing is, you never really know what's going to happen next. Because anything can happen. Good things, bad things. And scary, crazy things, when the world starts going all to pieces just when you least expect it.

14
Lady or the Tiger

I'm sound asleep when the horses scream. Dreaming I'm at this rodeo and I'm too small to look over the side, and there's just these big cowboy hats flying by, and I really want to see what's going on, and that's when all hell breaks loose.

The horses scream and Joe Dilly's feet hit the floor and he's standing over my bunk and shaking me. "Come on, Roy, there's something wrong!"

Them horses aren't in my dream at all. They really are going wild in the middle of the night.

Soon as I sit up there's a loud *crack* of thunder, sounds like a tree splitting. No lightning yet, but you can tell there's a storm coming fast across the sky.

Joe's pulling on his pants and boots and he's saying, "Where'd you leave that pony? In the barn or the corral?"

"The corral," I say, and that's when it hits me – all the noise is coming from the corral.

I'm at the door when Joe stops me and goes, "Better put on your pants."

So I do, only I get the legs crossed and I have to start over, and every time a horse screams it sounds like Lady, like she's dying, or being scared to death.

Which as it turns out is pretty close to the truth.

At first I can't see much of anything. Because the night is soaking up the lights from the bunkhouse, and the air is hot and thick and syrupy and hard to see through, and the noise from the scared horses comes from all around. Like I'm still asleep and sleepwalking or something.

Joe's there beside me and he goes, "It ain't just a storm coming, make them go crazy like this. Something else has got 'em riled. Maybe you better get back inside and let me handle it."

I pretend like I don't hear him, and then I scoot sideways around the corner of the building so he can't make me go back. Not with Lady in trouble.

I'm almost to the corral before I notice the cool dirt

under my feet. Forgot my boots. So I'm barefoot like a fool. And that's when I wonder: Was it another snake that has Lady and the horses in such a panic? Which makes me feel like each of my toes is a magnet for rattlers, and when I look at the ground my eyes play tricks and make me see snakey shapes slipping through the shadows, coming right at me.

I'm so scared I can't feel nothing, not even my feet.

The moon comes out of a storm cloud and there they are, all the horses in the corral reared up and going wild. Their eyes are dead white and crazy-mad and they're kicking their forelegs high in the air, like they want to scrape away the darkness and make it daytime.

Lady Luck is racing around in circles, going as fast as she can, and every few seconds she gives the rail a butt with her head. She's trying to bust out of that corral and she don't care what it takes.

I'm right there at the rail, watching her streak by but she don't see me, and there's no way I can think to stop her. Any second she might break a leg, or crash herself to death.

"Lady!" I'm shouting. "Stop! Please stop!"

Something sucks the air out of my lungs and the sky all at once goes *crack-crack-crack* like it's breaking all to pieces and the barns and the stables and the corrals and all the panic-crazy horses go frozen white for just a heartbeat as that first stroke of lightning takes the colour out of everything.

It ain't just rain comes down. More like a wave breaking from the sky, with water so thick in the air I still can't breathe, and the horses swimming in the dark, where all the colour has gone back into what you can't see.

There's mud everywhere and it sucks at my feet so I can't pick them up, but it don't slow Lady down – she's running like she wants to disappear. Which I would like to do except I can't move. Or maybe I'm not moving because my head is empty, like the crack of thunder erased my brain or something, and I can't seem to get thinking again.

What gets me moving is this: something big jumps over the fence rail, into the corral. At first I think it must be one of the horses, but it ain't as big as a horse, and then there's another flash of lightning turns everything white and I see there's a white tiger in with the horses.

A white tiger in there with Lady.

The lightning switches off and when I can see again, that tiger is still in the corral, shrieking and spitting at the horses.

Then Joe Dilly is beside me and he's pulling at me and saying, "That's a big old mountain lion! Keep out of there!"

That's when I see the tiger stripes are just streaks of mud and it really is a mountain lion. There's nothing else it could be, and it wants to kill the horses.

Joe's hands are all slippery with the rain and I manage to get away from him and run around to the other side of the corral. Because I want to open the gate and let Lady out, so she don't bust herself up or get eaten. I'm not really thinking about me or even about that big cat, all I'm thinking about is the pony.

"Lady!" I'm yelling. "This way! Over here!"

I lean under the rail and jerk up on my shoulder and sure enough the latch comes free and the gate swings open.

Somebody is yelling my name, it might be Rick, but I don't pay no attention. The only important thing is getting Lady away from that cat.

The horses get wind of me, or the gate being open, and all of a sudden they stampede for the opening. This crazy mess of hooves and heads and wild eyes and bone and muscle, all of it coming my way.

I throw myself back between the gate and the rail as the thunder goes by, and I can feel the air shaking with how scared they are, and I know they'd kill me if they could, because I'm not one of them, and right now they're scared to death of anything that isn't horse.

As those horses bust through the gate, breaking it to pieces, I end up face first in that sucking-down mud with the rain pouring all over me. But I don't care, because I figure Lady must have got away. Nothing can get her if she's running free.

But when I pry myself up from that mud and have a look, the cougar's still there, in the corral. He's got Lady cornered. She's trying to kick down the rail, but it won't go. The cougar knows what he's doing – he's got her so crazy with fear she can't think her way around him.

"Jump!" I scream. "Jump out of there!"

I know she could do it if she only knew how, but before she can move, the cougar is on her. He kind of slinks under her belly, keeping away from her feet. He reaches up and gets his claw into her flank and Lady cries out so bad it makes me weep.

Next thing I know I'm running into the corral with a piece of broken gate in my hand. Don't ask me what I'm going to do with that silly piece of wood because I don't know, I only want something in my hands.

The rain is streaking down and blurring everything and the cougar, it seems like he's part of the mud, the way he comes up out of the ground. Like the rain made him, or the lightning. He smacks Lady again with his paw and she goes down and I can see her wild eyes looking at me.

She wants me to do something, only I don't know what. So I'm screaming like a wild horse and kicking my hooves and swinging that little broken stick and making such a crazy fool of myself that the cougar finally notices.

He backs off of Lady where she's down in the mud, and he kind of slinks into himself and I can see his yellow eyes glowing in the rain. He's thinking what to do.

I'm going, "Get away from her! Go on, get out of here!"

Then I'm swearing like Joe Dilly, but the cougar don't care. His ears go back on his head and his lips pull back and he shows me all of his shiny teeth, and all of a sudden my throat feels like I swallowed a hot rock.

Next thing, somebody is shouting my name. It might be Joe, but I can't tell because I'm watching that cougar so hard.

I want to turn and run, but the mud won't let me, and so I have to keep cussing at the cougar, because if I stop I'll just fall down and give up. I can see how he's winding up and getting ready to jump at me. It's like he's getting thicker and more solid and his eyes are bigger and brighter, and I can smell how much he hates me. Hates me because I'm afraid, and because he's afraid, too.

He goes to jump and there's another *crack*, only this time it ain't thunder. The cat screams so hurt it makes my blood freeze up, and I don't want to look.

I can smell the gunpowder and when I open my eyes there's a dead thing in the mud and Mr. Jessup is on the other side of the corral, waving his rifle and calling my name.

"Get away from there, Roy! Go to your horse! Go to Lady!"

So I do it, I go to Lady. She's down in the mud, too, and bleeding from her flank, but she's alive, and she knows me, and that's all that matters.

15
Crazy as a Cougar

Mr. Jessup thinks the cougar was sick in the head.

"No mountain cat in its right mind would do what it did," he says.

We're all of us in the stable, me and Joe and Rick and Mr. Jessup, and Miss Lottie Davis, the horse doctor, she's come out in the middle of the night to tend to Lady.

That pony is hurting so much I can't help it, I'm crying as Dr. Davis sews up the claw marks the cougar left in her flank. "It might have had a brain disease," Dr. Davis says. She's stitching away like she's making a dress or something, except there's blood on her fingers. "Or it might be just plain crazy. That happens with big cats just like with people."

"Can a pony die from getting bit?" I ask.

"Don't you worry about your pony," she says. "She'll be fine."

But I catch the way she looks at Mr. Jessup and I know she's just saying that because she don't want to make me more upset than I am, which is plenty.

The only way to make Lady hold still is to tie her up in about nine directions, and her eyes are so big and round it hurts me, even though I'm not the one got raked open by a cougar. Dr. Davis says it's better not to knock her out, but I wish they would, so she don't have to feel that needle sewing her up.

Rick has come back from the main house with a bottle of liquor, and he pours some in paper cups for him and Mr. Jessup and Joe. "Just one to take off the chill," he says. "Man, I thought that boy was a goner. I really did."

They're all saying I must be crazy as that cougar, to run into the corral. They don't know I was scared out of my mind, which is different.

"Big cougar mauled a hiker, just a few months back," Dr. Davis says. "Might be the same animal."

"Might be," says Mr. Jessup. He keeps looking at me funny. He don't finish the booze in the paper cup, he's just holding it like he wants to be polite. His white hair's still wet from the rain, so you can see through it right to his scalp, but I still don't know what he's thinking. He looks at Joe and then he looks at me again and he goes, "Your brother told you to get back in the bunkhouse, right?"

"Yes, sir, he did."

"But you didn't."

"I had to help Lady," I say. "You understand about that."

"I do," he says. "But that doesn't mean you did the right thing. No horse is worth dying for, Roy. You don't believe me right now, but it's true."

"Darn right," says Joe. He's had two paper cups so far, and already you can see the difference in his eyes, the way they shine. "You get et up by a darn mountain lion, then where'd I be?"

Rick shakes his head and says, "Go on, give the boy a hard time, he deserves it. But I never saw no eleven-year-old kid take on a cougar that's bigger than two of him. And that's all I'll say on the subject."

Mr. Jessup looks at him and says, real quiet, "Put the bottle away," and he does.

Joe has that funny look he gets, and I see the way he'd like to mouth off to Mr. Jessup, but he catches sight of me and keeps his trap shut, and a few minutes later he says he might as well turn in.

"I'm staying here with Lady," I say.

Nobody says I can't, and the way I feel it wouldn't make any difference if they did, because they'd have to rope me up to get me out of that stall.

Dr. Lottie Davis stays on for a while after she finishes sewing up the wound. She sets on a fold-out stool she carries, and she just absolutely has to have a cigarette. "I'm supposed to have quit," she says. "But there's something about four o'clock in the morning calls that makes me crave nicotine, I guess."

"Is Lady going to be okay?" I ask.

Dr. Davis blows smoke out of her nose and looks at me for a long time. "You look so young, but you're not," she says. "Not where it counts."

"I been around for a while," I say.

"Uh-huh. Well, I guess I better talk to you like a grown-up, or you might corner me in a corral some dark and stormy night. The fact is, I'm fairly confident that your pony will recover. It looks worse than it is, really. But there's always a possibility of infection with a large animal wound. You never know what that cougar had on its claws."

"But you gave her shots for that, right? To make her heal?"

"Yes," says Dr. Davis. "But there's no guarantee, Roy.

Sometimes a viral infection gets into the blood and antibiotics don't help."

I go, "That's not going to happen to Lady. Nobody is going to hurt her again, not even a bunch of stupid germs!"

I don't mean to, but I guess maybe I'm shouting. Dr. Davis puts out her cigarette and gets up. She don't say nothing, but I get the idea she thinks I'm as crazy as that cougar, too.

16
The fever Poultice

I must have fell asleep, because the next thing I know, Joe is waking me up.

"Rise and shine, sports fans," he says, and his eyes are lit up like he's been awake for hours, or never went to bed at all. "Get some grub in your belly, you're going to need the strength."

I sit up and pull the hay out of my hair and right away I remember it's not a dream, the cougar really came into the corral and Lady really did get hurt.

She's just kind of standing there in her stall and not moving, like she's sleeping, except her eyes are open. She's quit tugging at the halter rig that keeps her from gnawing at her stitches. She don't even make her ears twitch when I call her name. She don't care about anything.

Joe, he's shoving a big plate of sausage and ranch eggs at me. "First things first," he says. "First you, and then your pony."

"Something's wrong with her," I say. "I ain't hungry right now."

"'Course something's wrong with her. We know that. And I don't care if you're hungry, you'll clean every crumb off this plate or else."

He don't say what else might be, but I take the food, and what do you know, I'm so hungry it makes me dizzy smelling the fried-up sausage and the butter on the toast. So I eat up, and fast.

Meantime Joe leans up against this post, drinking coffee from a blue Bar None mug, and he's looking at Lady. "The doc give her shots, did she?"

I got my mouth full, but I nod.

"I figured," Joe says. "Maybe it's the medicine makes her look dopey."

He's stroking Lady's nose and looking into her mouth and humming to himself like he does, and he's got this tight little smile on his face that means he don't like what he's seeing.

Soon's I finish eating I get right over there and

the first thing I notice is her breath smells funny.

"That's a fever smell," Joe says. "Any minute now she's going to break out in a sweat."

"What do we do?"

Joe shrugs. It's like he don't want to look me in the eye. "Wait it out. A fever will either break or it won't."

"I got to do something, Joe. I want to help her."

He don't say nothing for a while and then he says, "The vet done what could be done. Lady's got to help herself, Roy. An animal this sick, she's all sunk down inside herself, trying to get better."

"I can't just stand around and do nothing," I say.

"Then talk to her," he says, walking away. "It can't hurt."

At first I don't know what to say. When you think about it, it's pretty stupid, talking to an animal. But when Joe moves off to do his chores, I tell Lady what he's up to, and from there, well, I just keep on telling her things. Way back stuff, like how bad it was at the foster home, and how the other kids used to tease me about what a worthless drunk my real mother was before she died, even though I can't remember her at all, and how my father wasn't no better, and I'd get so mad I'd curl up inside my head and never say a word for weeks at a time, and the only thing kept me going there was thinking about this big brother I could hardly remember who was someday going to ride up on a black horse and rescue me, and one day he did, only it was an old pickup truck, not a horse. I'm telling Lady how the fire comes into Joe Dilly's eyes sometimes when he drinks, and gets us in trouble, and how we got to keep one eye on the road and the other for what's catching up behind us, and how I don't care about whatever bad things Joe might have done along the way, all that matters is we somehow found the Bar None, where everybody is welcome no matter what. I'm telling Lady she's got to sweat out this fever so she can run them cactus again, and be her old self. I'm telling her it don't matter none if she's a racing pony, who cares about some stupid old race, the only important thing is she gets better. I'm telling her maybe the summer will never end, and it won't matter what Sally Red Dawn does come fall, or what she finds out about me and Joe. Like Joe says, maybe pigs really *can* fly, sports fans, maybe me and Joe can stay in our own little bunkhouse where nobody can bother us, or make us do what we don't want.

Well, I keep talking until my throat's so dry the words disappear, and finally I notice that Lady ain't listening, she's all lathered up with the fever and her eyes have gone white and her knees are wobbly. I'm trying to find some spit so I can make my tongue work when all of a sudden her two front legs just fold up and she's down, and she lays there breathing so hard it hurts to hear it.

I'm trying to shout "Joe! Joe!" but nothing comes out, and so I run through the stable and into the shed until I find him bent over a fine Arabian. He looks up at me and he puts his file down and ties off the Arabian, and he takes off his leather apron.

"She's down with the fever, ain't she," he says.

All I can do is nod.

"Okay, you go get a bucket of water and a clean sponge. Make sure it's cool water. I'll meet you back at her stall."

I start to run for the bucket of water and Joe stops me. "Whatever happens, that's what's supposed to happen, you know what I mean?"

I shake him off and run for the water trough. I don't care what he says, the only thing that matters is Lady. I get the bucket and a brand-new sponge from the supply shed and when I get back to the stall, Joe is already there.

"Start with her withers," he tells me. "Sponge her down real gentle. I'll make sure her throat stays clear."

If you didn't know she was fever sick, you might think Lady had run about a hundred miles, the way she's lathered up. I start sponging off the sweat and she shivers at the touch. "Don't dip the sponge back in the bucket," Joe says. "Wring it out and start fresh each time. Go on, run back and get a fresh bucket."

Joe keeps me running until I'm pretty lathered up myself. Meantime he's got Lady's head in his lap and he keeps opening her mouth and making sure her throat stays clear, and once she nips his finger and draws blood. "Go on and bite me if you want," he says. "I don't mind."

We keep it up for a few hours, which seems like for ever, but the more I sponge off Lady, the worse she seems to get. At the start of it she was heaving and snorting to get her breath and now it's more like she's sighing, like she's giving up.

"We got to do something," I say. "We don't do something, she ain't going to make it."

Joe looks at me for a long time and then he says, "You take over on this end." He gets up and leaves me holding Lady's head in my lap. "I got an errand to run. I'll be back."

I feel like yelling and swearing at him for no good reason, but I don't. Joe goes off and there's just me and Lady Luck, and she seems like a goner for sure.

Maybe I'm sweet-talking her and maybe I'm not – I can't tell any more what's inside my head and what's coming out my mouth. But poor Lady is so choked up and wheezing she can't hear me anyhow, so what difference does it make? All I can think of is to whisper into her ear and go, "You're the best pony that ever was, you know that? Everybody thinks so. Mr. Jessup and Rick and Joe Dilly and me. The best that ever was, bar none."

After a time Joe comes back and he's got something in an old canvas bag. "Hey there, Roy, how you doin'?" he says, setting the bag down.

I don't say nothing, I'm waiting to see what he's got in the bag. Joe grins and gives me a wink and then he opens the bag and takes out this thick white cloth. Right away I can smell something powerful. Something like mint and pine sap and tar, only different.

"This here will do the trick," he says, unfolding the cloth. The stink gets stronger and Lady kind of whimpers – she can smell it, too.

"What is it, Joe?"

"They call it a poultice," he says. "A fever poultice."

"What's that?"

"From the old days," he says. "Before they had penicillin. You put this on the wound and it draws out the poison and cools the fever."

He unwraps the cloth, which looks like he tore up

a clean sheet, and there's gobs of this black, smelly goo, and when I ask him what's in it he shakes his head and says, "That's my secret. I will tell you there's pine tar. Some other powerful ingredients. A little Vaseline so it sticks. Nothing that can hurt her, if that's what you're worried about."

"I ain't worried about that."

"Okay then," he says.

He sets the poultice right on Lady's stitched-up wound, and then he wraps strips of sheeting around to hold it in place. Lady lifts her head and gives it a sniff and she falls back and starts wheezing again, like it hurts to breathe and she's tired of hurting.

"You make sure she don't shed the bandage," Joe says. "That's your job. I'll keep her sponged off."

The two of us work on her for hours and hours, until it comes round on night again. Me tending the bandage and Joe keeping her cool and seeing her throat is clear, and that she takes enough water. Once I'm sure she's up and died, but Joe makes me put my ear to her chest so I can hear her heart beating, and he tells me she's going to be okay. This is the worst, he says, and it'll get better.

"She's saving her strength," he says. "Sleeping. Which is what you should be doing, too."

"I better not."

"Go on," he says. "Lay down there in the hay beside her and catch a few winks. I'll be right here."

There's something about the way he says it that makes my eyes feel heavy, and I can't help it, the next thing you know Joe is tending me, fluffing up that hay like it was a real pillow, and I'm thinking they don't get any better than Joe Dilly, even if he does have the fire in his eyes sometimes. Then I'm fast asleep, just like that.

17
Joe Won't Go

When I wake up again there's light coming into the stables and right away I see that Lady's not in her stall. It's like somebody reared back and kicked me in the stomach, because what else can it mean except she's dead?

Then I hear Joe and Rick and Mr. Jessup talking, and I come running out of her stall and they're all of them way down at the other end of the stable, standing around like they haven't got a care in the world.

Joe has that same blue coffee mug and when he sees me he lifts it up and goes, "Look who's finally woke up."

I get to where they are, and that's when I hear her whinny and it goes right through me.

Lady Luck is alive and she's standing on her own four legs.

"We moved her down here so you could sleep where you were," Joe says. "Fever finally broke about four a.m. I guess a fever always breaks about that time of night, don't it, Rick?"

"Seems that way," he says.

I don't hear no more of what they're saying because I'm in there with her. I can't say anything, but she knows how I feel. After a while I hear Mr. Jessup cough and they all get out of there and leave us alone.

"I knew you'd be okay," I tell her, over and over again.

The truth is, I didn't know she'd be okay. I was only hopeful.

* * *

The days seem to speed up while Lady gets better, and I can hardly keep track of the time.

The pony can't do much while the stitches are healing, so Joe keeps me busy, and he's showing me a thing or two about shoeing horses.

"You ain't got the size for it right now," he says. "But you'll grow into it. You need to be certain in your mind what you're doing before you start anyhow. Brains first, muscles later."

He means you got to think about a job before you can do it. Already I know there's more to shoeing horses than fitting on the shoes. A lot of them Arabians don't even get shoes put on, they run barefoot in the pastures, but still you want to trim out their hooves or they'll splay or split or go lame. That's mostly what keeps Joe so busy, keeping up with them Arabians.

"You let a horse go natural, run in wild herds, in a few generations it'll lose size and turn mustang. For better or worse, horses are like they are because we made 'em that way, and that means you have to take care of 'em. See to their needs."

He's licking away with his big rasp file, studying each hoof like some people study books. Reading that hoof because there's a story in there, of how the horse grows and walks and runs, and what makes it feel good, and whatever ails it. You have to listen real close or you lose the sense of what he's talking about.

"You see this," he says, pointing at a low spot on the hoof wall. "You see this and you know why the conformation is off. The horse favours this spot and he loses the sense of his stride. The feel of his feet under him. He gets confused about how to move. He starts thinking, and when a horse starts thinking about how to walk or run, he's in real trouble. A horse has got to move by instinct or training or habit. That's why you look to the conformation."

When he says conformation, he means the way an animal looks and acts and how it feels about itself. The whole picture. All the parts working together. Joe Dilly, he can look at a horse that's standing still and know there's something wrong. Once he gets that horse moving, he knows how to put it right. Maybe it just needs a trim, or corrective shoes, or a particular kind of exercise, or a change in diet. Maybe it needs to be ridden, or could be it wants a rest.

"It ain't just nailing on a new shoe," he says. "Any fool can do that. Cowboys used to just bang 'em on and keep going. I hate to think how many fine saddle horses got ruined by store-bought shoes. They didn't know any better, them old cowboys. It ain't the feet you're fixing, it's the whole animal."

The thing of it is, I never seen Joe so easy or settled as he is at the Bar None. He don't even mouth off much to Mr. Jessup, when he usually hates most bosses like most people hate a splinter.

All he'll say about it is, "This place is okay." And he never mentions what will happen come the fall, which keeps getting closer and closer.

Rick and Mr. Jessup are real busy with Pit Stop, putting that champion roping horse through his paces, and even Joe has to admit the two of them know what they're doing. "I'll give him this – the man can handle a horse and rope," he says, watching from the barn one fine morning, and coming from Joe that's like saying he's practically the best in the world.

I tell Joe about how Mr. Jessup had a wife and son who died, but he already knowed it, and he don't care to speculate. And when I tell him how Mr. Jessup sometimes goes up to that old picnic spot on the bluff, and sits there alone on his horse, he says he don't want to hear it. Like the whole idea makes him nervous, which I can't understand. If it don't make Mr. Jessup nervous, why should it bother Joe Dilly? It's like he don't want to ever hear about anybody who died because it might be him someday.

Meanwhile Lady is getting stronger and pretty soon she's her old frisky self and I start riding her real easy around the ring. You can tell she wants to go, though. There's a lot of fast inside her wanting to get out, and I have to hold her back and say, "Easy there, girl. You're still mending, remember?"

I ain't thought much about the idea of racing her, one way or the other, until one evening Mr. Jessup comes into the stall when I'm running a currycomb over Lady, and he strokes his hand over where the cougar raked her and says, "That scar looks like a pink lightning bolt."

I look at the scar and he's right, it does look like a pink lightning bolt.

"How's she feeling?" he asks me.

"All the way back," I say. "Same as before."

"I thought as much," he says. "The thing of it is, we're shipping out for the state fairgrounds tomorrow. They got a rodeo and a horse race and there's room in the trailer for a pony just about this size."

He kind of catches me by surprise, but it don't take long before I like the idea.

"Can Joe come, too?" I ask.

Mr. Jessup don't even have to think about that. Right off he says, "Sure. I think he should be there."

But when I go running into the bunkhouse and tell Joe the news, he gets this frozen look on his face. "You go ahead," he says. "I'm busy."

"There's nothing can't wait," I say. "Is there?"

"You go on," he says. "I better not show my face around no rodeo. You never know who might be there."

Then he turns away and fiddles with stuff so he don't have to look at me.

18
A Proper Tent

Mr. Jessup says he ain't got no use for motels or RV trailers if he can help it, so we set up this tent, right there on the fairgrounds. It's a real nice tent, big enough to walk around inside, and better than a dingy little motel room, that's for sure.

"I never sleep so good as I do in a proper tent," Mr. Jessup says. He's standing there with his hands on his hips, looking everything over, making sure it's all trim and proper. "Night-time, the air is fresh and your mind is clear. Then, come the first ray of sun you're up and raring to go. Why, sometimes I think I should tear down the ranch house and put up a tent."

"Don't pay no attention to him," Rick says, winking at me. "The man would just as soon sleep on the ground as in a bed, that's how crazy he is."

Actually, there's real nice sleeping cots inside the tent, and even a small table and chairs. It's plenty civilized, except we got kerosene lanterns and no electricity. Also, if you camp out right there on the fairgrounds you get to stay near the horses. See, there's no room in the paddock, not with hundreds of animals brought from all over, so Pit Stop and Lady Luck have to stay in the horse trailer at night, and you can tell they don't much like it.

I ask Mr. Jessup, can Lady stay in the tent with us, but he don't take me serious. "Now, you want to sleep in the horse trailer, you can," he says. Then he goes to Rick, "They ever open this boy up, they're going to find he's made of hay and oats and saddle trees."

The sun's starting to go down by the time we get off the road and set up our stuff, and when Rick gets his barbecue fire going I'm so hungry I can feel it in my knees. Rick, he knows a thing or two about food, and he's got the coolers loaded up with ribs and 'taters and fresh corn, and some of them new peas you can eat raw, they taste so sweet.

You might think the smell of all those nervous animals would cut your appetite some, but it don't.

I eat so many of them barbecue ribs Rick says I must be growing a couple of extra ribs myself.

"The boy has the appetite of a sumo wrestler," he says. "I don't know where it all goes."

"Hollow leg," says Mr. Jessup.

"Maybe he's getting set to grow some," Rick says, looking me over.

Mr. Jessup shrugs and kind of squints at me. "Just so you don't grow much before the first race," he says. "Lady couldn't handle a rider much bigger than you, not if she's running for speed."

"Then I hope I never grow," I say.

The way they explain it, the race part is kind of separate from the rodeo, even though a lot of rodeo people are in on it. Mr. Jessup says it's the most disorganized race in six states, which is why everybody has such a good time.

"Any horse with four legs can enter," he says.

"Is there a prize?" I ask.

"There is, but you won't be winning much," he says. "Only a thousand dollars."

Only a thousand dollars! Well, I guess if you own the Bar None, a thousand dollars ain't much, but that's more money than me and Joe ever had altogether at one time. I figure, worse comes to worse and we have to hit the road again, a thousand dollars might buy a horse trailer for Lady, so she can come with us.

But Mr. Jessup, he don't seem to care if we win or not.

"You get your pony from the starting line to the finish without standing her on her head, you'll be a winner in my book," Mr. Jessup says.

"Nobody is going to beat Lady," I say.

"Too bad the boy don't have no confidence," Rick says.

Mr. Jessup uses a napkin to make sure there's no barbecue sauce on his face – he's a real careful eater – and he gives me some more of that squint of his. "She's never raced against another horse," he goes. "Let alone in front of a crowd of wild cowboys whooping it up. Maybe she won't want to go."

"She'll go," I say. "Soon's I yell 'Geronimo'."

I don't know why, but that makes Rick laugh. He's laughing so hard he chokes on his sparerib and we got to beat him on the back with our hats.

I'm so tired I can hardly keep my eyes open, but when I get in that cot, wouldn't you know, I keep thinking about Joe, back there on the Bar None, all on his lonesome.

I wish he was here in the tent, and I wish it so hard it won't let me sleep.

19
Mr. Jessup Gets a Haircut

You want to sleep late, don't camp out at no rodeos, because there's folks there who wake up the roosters.

I know because all of a sudden Rick is dragging me out of the cot in the middle of the night and going, "Come on, lazybones, time's a-wasting. Another hour and you'll miss the sunrise."

I go, "I seen it before," and try to put my head under the pillow, only he won't let me.

"You've got to take your pony to the beauty salon," he says. "Give her a new hairdo."

That don't make no sense at any time of day, but you can't ignore Rick when he's got a bee in his bonnet, so I get myself dressed and somehow get my boots on the right feet, and next thing you know he's shoving a mug of coffee in my hands and he goes, "I put three sugars in it, because you'll need the energy. Now you get over there and wake up your pony. Give her some sugar, too, if she wants it. I guess she don't drink coffee, does she?"

"Not so far," I say.

"Give her time," he says, and then he nose-laughs into his coffee mug like he does.

Lady is kind of fussy backing out of the trailer, and I got to calm her down some by sweet-talking her, but probably that's all the noise and commotion going on. Why, the sun ain't up yet and the whole place is going crazy! There's folks exercising their horses, and rat-eyed rodeo riders wandering around looking sick to their stomachs, and this Brahma bull bellowing from the stockade like he wants to stomp those cowboys into the ground, and RV generators that sound like jet-fired vacuum cleaners, and a bunch of dogs barking, and mosquitoes whining, and babies crying, and every other noise you can think of, all mixed together before you've had breakfast.

It turns out Rick ain't kidding about the beauty parlour for horses. They got this stall set up where you bring your horse and they take care of the brushing and grooming and shampooing, and trim the mane and tail, and do most everything, Rick says, except dab it with French perfume.

They get done with Lady and she looks brand-new pretty, and the funny part is, she knows it. She flicks her tail so high and mighty I go, "Yes, your highness. Is it okay if we go back to the trailer – excuse me, your castle?" She snorts and stamps her foot and makes up for it by nuzzling me with her nose as if she wants to say: See, it's really me.

They can't do nothing about covering up her scar, though. A scar like that is for ever, Mr. Jessup says, only he calls it a badge of honour.

"It proves she has a heart," he says. "A lot of other ponies would have just up and died, but I guess you know that."

"Yes, sir, that's what I figured, too."

I don't see Mr. Jessup around while Rick is busy getting breakfast ready. He's taken Pit Stop out to the roping ring, letting him get used to the place. Only Rick says it's as much Mr. Jessup getting used to it as the horse.

"That man looks like he don't have a nerve in his body, but he does. He must, right? He didn't, he wouldn't be human."

"I guess," I say.

That's when Mr. Jessup sneaks up on us. "What are you all guessing at?" he asks.

"Oh, nothin'," says Rick. "You ready for sausage and scrambled eggs?"

Mr. Jessup says he don't have much of an appetite, and when he hears that, Rick looks at me and winks. I guess there must be something wrong with me, because race or no race, I'm so hungry I end up eating Mr. Jessup's share, which he don't mind at all.

"I'm feeling poorly," he says to Rick.

Rick says, "You always feel poorly before an event, Nick. You'll be okay once you get the horse under you and the rope in your hands."

"I suppose," says Mr. Jessup, like he don't believe it for a minute.

They got enough stuff going on at this rodeo to fill up three whole days, but wouldn't you know, the calf-roping event is the very first morning, which means we can't mess around, we got to get Pit Stop ready to go.

"Tell you what," Rick says to Mr. Jessup. "You go on into town and get a haircut."

"I don't need a haircut," says Mr. Jessup.

"I know that," Rick says. "But do it anyway. Just so you don't think about roping for a few minutes. When you get back, all you got to do is climb on your horse and go."

When Mr. Jessup is gone, Rick makes a show of mopping his brow and goes, "Whew! Okay, you want to go watch the show, go ahead."

"But I thought we had a lot of work to do," I say. "Getting his horse ready."

"The horse is ready. I just wanted to keep Nick moving. He stands around, he'll think himself into doing something wrong. Some ways there ain't much difference between a man and a horse."

Well, what happens is this. I'm right there hanging on the rail when the show starts. First thing they have this parade. All these duded-up folks come riding through the ring on horseback. They got pretty girls in sparkly costumes holding these big flags that whip in the wind, and a lot of ornery-looking cowboys with their chests all puffed out like they're going to get a medal, and they got a sheriff with a big white Stetson hat, and a rock 'n' roll singer who can't remember all the words to the National Anthem, but what I notice most is the clowns.

I seen rodeo clowns on TV, of course, but it looks different when you're close up and in person. What they got to do is look funny, act stupid, and save people's lives – all at the same time. The way it happens, say this bronco comes busting out of the chute, and before you can blink your eyes the rider comes flying off and he's down in the dirt with the horse trying to stomp him into a thousand pieces. Well, that clown in the baggy pants, he's got to get the horse away from the rider it wants to kill. And he's got about two seconds to do it or there'll be blood in the dirt. It's like magic, how they keep on going and how they trick them kill-crazy animals.

If you think the broncos are scary, though, you should see the bulls! And these ain't just normal bulls, which are bad enough, these are the meanest Brahma bulls they can find. Them bulls are made of pure steam. If a bull don't want to turn a rider into hamburger, it don't get into the rodeo. And all you get to hold on to is a little bitty piece of rope, with one hand. No saddle, no stirrups or nothing. Just you and a thousand pounds of muscle and horn.

Rick says the bull riders are as crazy as the bulls. Why else would a man get up on an animal that hates him, and then try to make the thing mad enough to turn itself upside down and inside out before it tries to kill you?

This one bull, he comes flying out of the chute, trying to climb straight up in the air, and the rider, he's getting shook up so bad his brains turn to jelly and he forgets how to let go of the rope. They got to rescue him by horseback, and then the bull *really* gets mad and charges this padded barrel where the clown is hiding, and butts the barrel so hard it smacks up against the side of the ring and the poor clown crawls out rubbing his head.

Rick says people working in the rodeo call 'em bullfighters, not clowns, which makes sense.

I seen one jump over the horns and get his pants torn up, right where it hurt! This stuff ain't fake like the movies or wrestling, it really happens. Most of them riders and bullfighters ain't got a bone they haven't busted, and they got this funny look in their eyes, like they been to the moon or something.

The next thing happens is what they call the bull-dogging event. There ain't any Brahma bulls, though, they're regular steers. What happens is the dogger, he chases the steer, jumps down from his horse while it's still running hell-bent for leather. Then he grabs the steer by the horns and wrestles it to the ground. They time him with a stopwatch and the fastest man wins. I heard he might win as much as five hundred dollars – I don't know what they give the steer, but he seems to get the worst of it.

Anyhow, I'm having so much fun I clean forget about Mr. Jessup and his roping horse. Then I see him across the ring, all duded up in a black Stetson hat and a fancy shirt, and he's moping along beside Pit Stop like he forgot to do his homework or something. You'd think he's on his way to the dentist to get all his teeth pulled, that's how long his face is.

I run under the stands and catch up to him just as he and Rick and the horse get to the grate behind the roping chute.

"I can see you're all tense and nervous in anticipation of your race," Rick says to me.

"What?" I say. "Oh, that race."

"Let that be a lesson," Rick says to Mr. Jessup. "The wisdom of the innocent."

"Shut up," Mr. Jessup says, real quiet.

I never heard him say that before, so I know he's nervous. Rick keeps making jokes, but Mr. Jessup, he don't crack a smile. He don't look at nobody, just at his hands, like he's never seen 'em before.

I can't see what's going on past the roping chute, but the crowd is cheering, so the other ropers must be doing okay. Rick is fussing around with Pit Stop, checking to see the saddle cinches are tight, and the stirrups are right, and then he hands the lariat rope to Mr. Jessup and says, "You're up."

Mr. Jessup, he gets up on his horse like he figures he'll be shot any second now. Then Rick fixes the shorter piece of rope in his belt and slaps him on the back. "Go get 'em," he says. "Don't think about it, just do it."

The whole idea about roping is, you got to keep as close as you can to the calf. There's this open stall for the roping horse and right next to it is this gate for the calf, and the horse gets right up next to where the calf is waiting, bawling and nervous and wanting to run. Then when the rider is ready to go, he nods to the gate man and they spring loose that calf and a good roping horse is right on top of it as it comes out of the chute.

Pit Stop, he sticks so close to the calf you'd think he was more cow than horse. Before you know it, Mr. Jessup has dropped a loop over the calf's head and then Pit Stop, he puts on the brakes so hard you can almost hear the screech. The rope tightens up and the calf goes down and Mr. Jessup comes flying out of the saddle with the other rope in his teeth and he's down in the dirt whipping that rope around the calf's legs so fast his hands are blurred. A machine couldn't have done it quicker.

Why, the whole thing is over so fast I ain't had time to take a breath or swallow, and Rick is leaning beside me at the gate, chuckling the way he does and nodding his head.

Mr. Jessup comes back out of the ring dusting his chaps with his hat and that old regular smile is back on his face. "You see that horse work that calf?" he says.

138

Rick says, "I guess you didn't do nothing, huh? Just along for the ride?"

"That's about the size of it," he says.

Then they're both looking at me, kind of staring.

"What?" I say. "What?"

"Better get the saddle on Lady Luck," Mr. Jessup says. "You're next."

20
The Crazy Wind
Keeps Roaring

What happened was, Mr. Jessup lost the roping contest to this other guy by one-tenth of a second. It'll take you longer than that to blink your eyes, so that's how close he come. The thing is, he seems really happy even though he didn't win.

"We'll get 'em next time," is all he'll say about it.

He and Rick walk with me and Lady to where they're having the race. This is outside the rodeo part, on a stretch of dirt track with these rickety-looking grandstands on either side. They got this old starting gate they tow around on a tractor. The thing about a quarter-mile racetrack, it just goes flat out and straight – there's no curve to it.

"Race a Thoroughbred around an oval track, you have to risk your life fighting for position. You have to get inside along the rail," says Mr. Jessup. "In a straight-ahead race like this, all you have to do is hang on and let the horse run."

"And steer clear of other horses," says Rick. "Pretend they're cactus and you'll be fine."

You never seen such a mess of horseflesh milling around raring to go. There's so many horses entered they got to have a bunch of races because they won't all fit in the starting gate at the same time. Then the next day they have another race, with all the winners, to see who's got the fastest horse of all.

"Don't worry about that," Mr. Jessup says. "Take it one race at a time."

"We got you in for the third heat," Rick says. "That way you'll have a chance to see how they do it, but the track won't be too messed up."

I figure Lady is the one who should watch, since she's going to do the racing part, so I take her under the grandstands, where we can see out through to the track. It's kind of cool and dim and private feeling under there, like we found a secret place all to ourselves. You can hear all the people squirming around on the seats above us and tapping their feet.

It turns out this was a pretty dumb idea, going under the stands, because we can't really see that good. All I know is, this bell rings and then a couple seconds later a bunch of horses gallop by, so close together it looks like they'll get tangled up for certain. Only somehow they don't. A moment later and everybody is cheering.

Lady, she sees all them horses running and she starts to snort and paw her front feet, like she's trying to tell me something. 'Course you can't really know what she's thinking, but I figure she wants to get out there and go fast, just like the other horses.

When we come back out from under the grandstand, Rick is hopping up and down and cursing. "They can't do it!" he's saying. "It ain't fair! What's his age got to do with it? Have you seen him ride? Have they?"

Mr. Jessup catches sight of me and he says, "Wait here." Then he stalks off with his fists balled up and shoved in his back pockets.

"What's wrong?" I ask.

"They went and changed the rules," Rick says. "Now they say all riders have to be at least fifteen."

I guess I didn't know how much I wanted to race until they took it away, because it feels like someone punched me hard in the stomach. I don't know whether to swear or start crying. Rick, he feels so miserable rotten he can't even look me in the eye. "Somebody is always making up new rules," he says. "Ain't we got enough rules in the world already?"

Even Lady looks sort of mournful, and she puts her head down and nuzzles at me, like she wants me to feel better. I'm about ready to take the saddle off her and lead her back to the trailer when Mr. Jessup comes loping back. He's got his hands out of his pockets but you can't tell what he's thinking from the look on his face.

"Well?" Rick says.

"Better get up on your pony, Roy. Your race starts in five minutes."

Mr. Jessup won't say what he done to make it okay, but I figure he just squinted extra hard and they changed their minds.

He opens his mouth like he's got something even more important to tell me, but then he changes his mind and pats Lady on the rump and says, "Don't you worry about anything. Just stay on the horse."

When I get over to the starting gate, it hits me that Lady is the only pony-sized horse in the race. The rest of them are all quarter horses, either purebred or mixed with Thoroughbred blood for speed.

"Wait here," Mr. Jessup says. "We'll check out your gate."

He and Rick go off. All the other riders are bigger than me and I can't really see what's going on. This scrawny, long-necked guy pulls his horse alongside and stares down his nose at me and Lady. His eyes are small and mean and look kind of like little wet marbles stuck in his face. After a while he says, "You must be in the wrong place, sonny. This is the quarter mile."

"I know what it is," I say.

"This ain't a pony race for kids," he says.

"I know that, too," I say.

He stares at me some more with those mean little eyes and then he makes a pruny face and goes, "Just keep out of my way, sonny. You got that? Let the real horses race."

Without me asking her to, Lady turns around and lifts her tail and leaves a pile of fresh horse buns right next to him. Like she's saying, That's what I think of you, mister. A couple of other riders see her do it and they start laughing and one of them goes, "Hey, Mullins, you're hip-deep in horse-pucky again!" And Mullins, he looks over at us and sniffs like he smelled a bigger stink than Lady made and you just know how he hates us for sure now.

I back up and try to keep clear of him, but Lady, she has ideas of her own, like she's sassing him, until he finally reaches out and flicks her nose with the tip of his boot. Before I can say anything, he leans over and keeps his voice real low, so nobody else can hear. "Keep that nag away from me, kid, if you know what's good for you."

It ain't the first time I been threatened, but the way he says it scares me some. Like he knows stuff I don't and can make things happen to me.

Suddenly Rick is there and he goes, "You seen a ghost, kid? You're looking awful pale."

I shake my head. Next thing I know Rick is leading Lady up to the gate with all the other horses and Mr. Jessup is there, helping to shoo her in. The trouble is she don't want to go. You can't blame her, she's never seen a starting gate before, or been around so many nervous horses all at once.

Well, what happens is I'm still thinking about what that creepy Mullins said when the bell goes off and the gate pops open.

All of a sudden there's a cloud of dust in my eyes. The other horses are out of the gate and running hard, and me and Lady are left behind, standing still.

From the grandstands I can hear people laughing and hooting and yelling stuff like, Hey, lookit the kid on the pony!

Finally it comes to me what I'm supposed to do,

so I slap the reins and yell *"Geronimo!"* at the top of my lungs.

You already know about Lady and how she loves to run, and how fast she is from a dead start. Well, she takes off like a high-power rifle bullet, so quick and sudden I almost get jerked backwards out of the saddle.

I never even touch her with the spurs. Lady's running so smooth and perfect it's like I'm hanging on to the top of a rocket that keeps going faster, the faster it goes. I crouch down and bury my head in her neck because the wind is so strong in my face, so I can't really see what happens next.

All I know is, Lady is running through traffic. There's horses right up along both sides of us and she's weaving around 'em like she did those cactus. She's going so fast she's stretched out flat and low to the ground, and the other riders are blocking out the light.

We're in the dark between pounding horses with wild eyes.

It's almost as dark as it was under the grandstands. I can't hear nothing but the thump of my own heart. I can feel Lady's heart, too, the same as mine.

It's like everything slows down the faster we go.

I forget to breathe. I forget about everything. I even

forget about winning the race. All I'm thinking about is sticking on that saddle!

Next thing I know, we're breaking into daylight, and all of a sudden this huge roar comes up.

At first it sounds like a crazy wind, the way it'll come through an old barn and put the chills up your back. I pull back on the reins and Lady starts to slow down but the crazy wind keeps roaring.

Then Rick and Mr. Jessup come running. They're both huffing and puffing and out of breath. They got these funny looks on their faces and it makes me think that something bad happened.

"What's wrong?" I say. I have to shout because that crazy wind keeps on roaring.

Mr. Jessup catches up to us and takes Lady's halter by the hand, holding her still. He's still panting some. "Wrong?" he says. "There's nothing wrong."

"He don't know," says Rick.

Then Mr. Jessup says, "I never saw anything like it in my life. You came from behind and you won."

That's when I figure out that the crazy wind is the crowd cheering us.

"It wasn't me," I say. "Lady did all the running."

21
Finger-Pointing

It ain't much fun being famous. We can't even eat our supper without people coming up to the fire and asking can they see the lightning-fast filly that got mauled by a cougar, and the boy who rides her. The first couple of times, Mr. Jessup explains everything real polite, and introduces me around, but after a while I just go and stay inside the tent because the whole thing makes me a lot more nervous than being in a race.

Rick sticks his head in the tent flap one time and goes, "Can I have your autograph?" and I have to throw a chicken wing at him to make him stop.

That guy Mullins comes by after the sun is all the way down. He just gives me a look like he's got something stuck in his throat, then he takes Mr. Jessup aside. They're standing over where Lady is staked out, munching on a bit of green hay we put down, and Mullins keeps pointing at Lady. Jabbing his finger at her.

Mr. Jessup, he's standing there listening but his face is real quiet and he's not saying much. Finally Mullins pokes his finger at Mr. Jessup's chest and the next thing you know Mr. Jessup has grabbed hold of that finger and Mullins's face is all scrunched up like he wants to scream but he don't dare.

Soon as Mr. Jessup lets go of that finger, Mullins takes off like a scalded cat.

"I see you and Mouldy Mullins are making friends," Rick says when Mr. Jessup comes back to the fire.

Mr. Jessup turns to me and goes, "Did that man try to interfere with you today?"

I shrug. "Not exactly," I say.

It turns out Mr. Molton T. Mullins owns a big ranch that borders the Bar None, and Mr. Jessup says he's a troublemaker. One of his best quarter horses won a heat, and he'll be riding it in the final race tomorrow.

"He figures his horse'll be worth a whole lot more if he wins. My impression is, he's worried about getting beat by Lady," says Mr. Jessup. "Wants her out of the race on a technicality."

"And what kind of technicality would that be?" Rick asks.

"That she's a pony, not a legal-sized horse at all."

Rick makes a snorting noise and stirs a stick in the fire like he's looking for something hidden in the ash. "He's talking through his hat. This particular race is open to all comers. Always has been. That's the beauty of it."

"Mullins doesn't see it that way."

"Uh-huh," says Rick. "I noticed you give him a little advice on what to do with that finger of his."

"My mother always said it was rude to point at folks," says Mr. Jessup.

A while later, this group of ranchers comes by and they talk real soft with Mr. Jessup. One of 'em writes stuff down in a little notebook. Before they go, everybody shakes hands and when Mr. Jessup comes back to the fire he's grinning like a kid.

"The race just get more interesting?" Rick asks him.

"You might say that."

"Let me guess. You're betting against Mullins's horse."

But Mr. Jessup don't want to talk about it. He says I better turn in and try to get some shut-eye.

Soon as I fall asleep, I have this dream that Joe comes into the tent. He's standing there in the dark with his hat in his hands, watching me sleep. He never says a word, but I can feel him making sure I'm okay.

22
Go, Lady, Go

If you ask me, they must give out crazy pills before a big race. Because all the folks jammed into the grandstands are just going nuts. They're screaming and hollering and waving flags and carrying on like this was Christmas and the Fourth of July and everybody's birthday all rolled into one.

Rick has to talk loud so I can hear him over the crowd. "There's only one thing for you to worry about," he says.

"I know."

"Getting a clean start."

"I know."

"I know *you* know. What I'm worried about is your pony. Does *she* know?"

Just then Mr. Jessup comes by and lays his hand on Rick's shoulder. "Leave the boy alone," he says. "He'll do what he has to do. Won't you, Roy?"

My throat has dried up, which makes it hard to get the words out, so I nod my head.

"You'll be fine," Mr. Jessup says. He stops tugging on the rim of his hat and cocks his ear. "You hear that?"

You can't hear much other than the crowd raising a ruckus, but then I figure out that's what he means – what the crowd is making so much noise about.

The whole bunch of 'em are yelling out this chant:
Geronimo! Geronimo!
Go, Lady, go!
Geronimo! Geronimo!
Go, Lady, go!
"I guess they want you to win," says Mr. Jessup.

Rick, he's shaking his head and staring at the grandstands. "I never heard nothing like it," he says. "Feels like an ice cube run right up my spine."

They're chanting so loud we almost don't hear the announcement about getting to the starting gate. A lot of the horses are so nerved up by the noise there's almost a stampede. This one real pretty quarter horse, his eyes are rolling white, and the rider can't get him turned no matter how hard he tries. They finally have to lead him away.

What with all the horses backing around and bumping each other behind the starting gate, Lady and me get separated from Rick and Mr. Jessup. The next thing you know, that guy Molton T. Mullins is nudging us from behind. He's pulling so hard on the reins his horse is bleeding around the bit.

"How do," he says. "No hard feelings, I hope."

His long bony face is smiling but I don't trust him. Before I can turn away, he's reaching down and messing with Lady, rubbing her flank and stroking the saddle blanket and fiddling around where I can't see him. "Nice rig," he says, but you can tell he don't mean it. "Nick Jessup give you that, too?"

I don't want to tell him nothing so I don't.

There's Rick and Mr. Jessup waving at me at the other end of the starting gate. I'm heading over there when all of a sudden this hand comes out of the crowd and grabs Lady by the hackamore.

"Just a minute, sports fans."

Why, it's Joe Dilly! He's standing there big as life and he's got on a brand-new ivory-button shirt and clean dungarees and his best hat, and his go-to-church boots are all shined up.

"Joe! I thought you wouldn't come!"

He puts his finger on the side of his nose and grins up at me. "Changed my mind. Now tell me quick, who was that man just now, messing with your saddle?"

I tell him about old Mouldy Mullins, and how he's afraid we might beat his horse, and that he's acting friendly but he don't mean it.

"Is that a fact," says Joe.

He ducks under Lady and the next thing I know he's tightening up the saddle cinch.

"There," he says, giving Lady a pat on the rump. "You'll be okay now."

So Mullins tried to loosen my saddle!

I swear there must be smoke coming out of my ears by the time I get Lady over to where Rick and Mr. Jessup are waiting by the starting gate. I'm so mad I forget to tell them what happened, or how Joe fixed it.

The next thing I know, that bell is ringing and the gate pops open and the big surprise is how *Geronimo!* comes out of my mouth without me even thinking about it.

We get a clean start, just like Rick wanted. Lady bolts out of there so quick I swear you can hear her burning rubber. You don't even have to touch her with the spurs because there's nothing she likes better than going fast.

For about six heartbeats I can't see nobody up with us.

We're out ahead!

And then the shadows come up from behind and there's pounding horses all around us and I can hear the riders panting like they were horses, and the horses are wheezing like people.

I shake the reins and yell for Lady to go faster and she does. She's stretched out like a bird skimming up from the water and for a little while we pull clear ahead again, and I can see the blur of faces in the grandstands. I can't hear nothing, though – it's like I got mufflers on my ears and all I can hear is the blood pounding in my head.

Then – *wham!* – something hits me from behind and I start to fall. I catch a glimpse of this mean grinning face – Mullins! – he's banged his horse into Lady and yanked me loose from the saddle!

I'm slipping down sideways and I'm backward dizzy, but my sleeve catches on the horn of the saddle and my left foot is stuck in the stirrup and I'm hanging on for dear life. Lady can see me and feel where I am and I can tell she wants to stop so I don't get hurt, but I'm so mad at Mullins I'd rather get run over than quit.

"Go!" I'm saying to her with my arms around her

neck. She's watching me talk to her and she hears me. "Go! Go! Go!"

And then we're flying, oh yes. It's like Lady sprouts these invisible wings or something, and the wind she makes is lifting us up.

I'm swung all the way round so I'm under her neck and I can feel her muscles kind of rippling and moving under her skin. It feels exactly right. Everything matches. Her muscle and bone and her hooves and the way her eyes watch me. I can feel her saying, *We're flying now, boy! Watch us go!*

Suddenly there's daylight all around us again and I'm hanging upside down under the fastest pony in the whole wide world and I catch sight of Joe Dilly standing on the rail as we go by. He's whooping it up and waving his hat and he looks so happy for once in his life that I forget what I'm doing and almost let go.

But I don't let go. I keep hanging on.

The next thing you know another one of the riders comes alongside and grabs me by the belt and lifts me back into the saddle and he raises my hand in the air and I can't hear nothing because the blood is still up in my ears but I can tell from the way folks are looking at me what happened.

We won.

Later on, somebody tells me the whole race took only about twenty seconds from start to finish, but that don't tell the truth of how long it lasted, or all the things that happened.

Soon's we cross the line it seems like everybody pours out of the grandstands and it gets so thick with folks that nobody can move. It's like they all want to touch Lady Luck, and me, too, and Lady don't like it much but we're so jammed in she can't do nothing about it.

"Roy! Roy!"

That's Mr. Jessup yelling, and he's climbing over people until he gets near us, then he starts pushing at folks with his Stetson hat until he clears a space around us and we manage to get over into the paddock somehow.

Once we got clear, Mr. Jessup lifts me out of the saddle and gives me a quick hug and he goes, "I thought you were a goner, son."

"Lady wouldn't let me fall," I say.

Then I go, "Where's Joe?"

Mr. Jessup looks around but we can't spot Joe Dilly nowhere. Then I see where Mullins is at – he's still on his horse, trapped in the crowd like he can't get into the paddock. There's folks yelling and waving their fists at him and his face is red and shiny and you can see where his mouth is shrunk up because he's mad about losing.

That's when I see Joe. He's there in the crowd and the next thing you know he's yanking Mullins out of the saddle – just like Mullins yanked me – and he's dragging him down into the crowd and then I can't see what happens next.

I hear the sirens, though, and see the way the crowd kind of melts around the police cars as they come through with their lights flashing.

They say it took a bunch of sheriff's deputies to hold Joe down. They say he was crazy and wild and out of his head, and that if the law didn't stop him he might have killed Mullins.

That's what they say. All I know is, when Joe gets busted, that's when all the bad things start catching up, and the fire comes back in Joe Dilly's eyes, and pretty soon the whole world goes up in flames.

23
Joe Dilly Stayed Too Long At The Fair

"The way I see it, Mullins deserved to get the tar kicked out of him," says Rick. "He's a liar and a cheat and it's about time somebody took him down a peg."

He's looking straight ahead and driving with both hands on the wheel. There's just me and him in the truck, towing the horse trailer home. Mr. Jessup has stayed back to see about getting Joe sprung from jail.

When I don't say anything about what happened, Rick says, "Penny for your thoughts."

I go, "Nothing. That's what I'm thinking about – nothing."

Rick thinks for a while and then he reaches over

and pats my hand and says, "Nick'll take care of it. Why, they'll probably beat us to the Bar None."

I figure he's just trying to make me feel better, but wouldn't you know it, by the time we back the trailer up to the stable, this sheriff's car with a gold star painted on it comes skidding down the fire road, kicking up rooster tails, and it stops in the main yard.

You can't see through the windows, but when the doors open, there's Mr. Jessup and Joe and the sheriff getting out, and they're all shaking hands and smiling at each other like they just come back from a party.

I run up to Joe, but before I can say anything he shushes me.

"Not now, Roy," he says.

I try to hug him but he's so stiff he won't hug.

The sheriff, he tips his hat and shoots Mr. Jessup a look, and then he gets back in his car and pretty soon all you can see is the dust it makes leaving.

"It's over," Mr. Jessup says to Joe. "Let it go."

"That stinking son of a scum," says Joe.

At first I think he's cursing the sheriff, but he means Mullins, the man he hit.

Joe kicks at the dirt and stalks off to the bunkhouse.

Mr. Jessup looks at me and says, "Your brother is a hothead, but I guess you know that."

"I'd a done the same thing," says Rick.

Mr. Jessup says, "It doesn't matter what you might have done in the same situation, Rick. Joe's the one in trouble. Mullins won't drop the charges. He won't take money and he won't listen to reason."

I run into the bunkhouse, looking for Joe. He's got his cot tipped over and stuff from his kit bag strewn around and he's looking for something. He finds it – this pint whisky bottle he must have hid there, but when he lifts it up to the light the bottle is empty.

"Aw nuts. Can't a man get a drink around here? Can't he?"

"Joe, please. Mr. Jessup will fix things."

"Is that what you think?"

"He fixed it so I could get in the race. He can fix old Mullins, too. You just got to give him a chance."

Joe sprawls out in the mess he's made. He's got a hand over his face like he don't want me to see his eyes. "Listen to me, Roy. That sheriff let me go because Nick Jessup wanted him to, but it ain't going to end there. He's going to check up on me. You know what that means, don't you?"

I know what that means but I don't want to think about it. I just want everything to stay the same. Me and Joe living here at the Bar None, and riding Lady Luck and everything.

Except we can't. And I know what we have to do.

"We better get out of here, Joe," I say. "Hit the road and don't look back."

Joe lifts his hand away from his eyes and looks at me for a long time. "Too late for that, kid brother. Like the song says, I stayed too long at the fair."

I don't want to hear about no stupid old song that Joe Dilly carries around inside his head. So I start packing up his bag, and mine, too, and I'm talking real fast so I don't have to think about what I'm saying. It just runs out of my mouth.

"Go on, get your stuff together, Joe, we're out of here. Why, it's the best thing ever happened, leaving this stupid old ranch. I don't care if I never see another fancy Arabian prancing around like he's something special. We'll find us a place where they ain't got rattlesnakes or mountain lions or thunderstorms, or crazy stallions like Showdown. I just won a thousand dollars, Joe. Maybe we can put it down on a place of our own! Rick says they still got cheap land down in Mexico, that's what we'll do, we'll head south. Yes sir! We'll keep on going till we hit a place where a thousand dollars can buy a ranch as big as this one, and you can be the boss, Joe, it'll be just you and me and a few horses that hardly need shoeing. Just enough so you can keep your hand in. Friendly horses that won't bite you or kick you or step on your feet.

Joe? Remember what you said, that night up on the mountain? How we could be kings? How we could be princes? Well we *can* – we just got to get out of here while the getting's good."

I don't even know what kind of silly stuff I'm spouting, but it kind of freezes Joe where he is, and he quits looking for whatever other booze he thinks he hid, and he's staring at me with those soft eyes of his, and after a while he nods and says, "Okay, here's the plan. You finish packing up those bags. I'm going to go gas up the pickup and I'll be back for you. How about that?"

"It won't take a minute, Joe. I'll come with you."

"Naw, let's do it right. Get all our gear together. We're going to need it when we get that ranch, right? Right?"

I run to the bunkhouse door and Joe grins at me and ruffles up my hair like he does and he says, "Hang in there, sports fans. I'll be right back."

I watch Joe Dilly drive that old Ford pickup off the Bar None, and the whole time I know he ain't coming back for me. Maybe he figures I'll be better off without him. Or maybe he's fixing to go crazy and he don't want me around when it happens.

24
The Sparks Fly Up
Like Birds On Fire

I'm out in the stable with Lady. Not talking to her like I sometimes do, just sitting around and waiting, because you never know, Joe might change his mind and come back, and that's when I smell it.

Smoke.

It's like a flavour in the air. Not close-by smoke, but real thin smoke from somewhere far off in the distance. Smoke you can't see yet. All you can do is taste it on the bitter part of your tongue.

I run out of the stable and look but I can't see the fire.

Rick comes out of the main house and sniffs around and says, "Where's Joe at?"

I tell him Joe went to gas up the truck and Rick gets

this worried look, but he don't say anything, he just goes back in the main house.

I stay out in the yard, waiting. It's night now, but you can still see where the mountains are darker along the edge of the sky, and where the stars are starting to come through like somebody's making pinholes up there to let the light back in.

I'm waiting so hard I can't move, not even when I hear that first siren that sounds like a baby crying as it goes by, or the phone ringing mean and angry in the main house, or the sound of Mr. Jessup's boots coming outside to find me.

"They've got big trouble at the Mullins ranch," he says. "Somebody set fire to the hay field. They, ah, the fact is, they say they spotted Joe's truck in the general vicinity. You know anything about that?"

"He won't hurt the horses," I say real quick. "He never hurts the horses."

"What are you talking about, Roy?"

But I don't want to talk and he don't make me. He's just out there in the night with me, leaning against the fence rail and not talking, but he knows. He don't have to say it. You can tell by the way he leans against the fence that he knows Joe Dilly done it this time.

Before long it starts glowing pink along the horizon,

but it's not the sun coming up. What happens is light from the brushfire gets reflected in the clouds. If you don't know what you're looking at, you might think it was real cheerful and pretty. But it ain't.

After a while the phone rings again and then Rick comes running out. He hasn't gone far but already he's out of breath. "The wind went and shifted," he says. "It's coming our way!"

Mr. Jessup gets up quick from where he's setting against the fence rail. "The ground is tinder dry between here and the Mullins place," he says. "Get the horses out of the stables. Put 'em all out in the holding corral."

Rick's already running for the trailers, getting the rest of the ranch hands to help him with the horses. I go into the stable with Mr. Jessup and we bring out Pit Stop and Lady and walk them down to the big corral.

Mr. Jessup says there's hardly a blade of grass left in the corral, so the ground won't burn under their feet.

"Can't they just run away?" I ask.

"A horse can outrun a brushfire," says Mr. Jessup. "But it can't outthink it. You put horses and fire together, the fire usually wins. They'll be safe enough here, no matter what burns."

Rick and the hands come through, easing the Arabians along a few at a time, like there's nothing wrong. But they know. They can smell it coming.

They never put all the horses together in that one corral before, and there's so many there's hardly room to move. But Rick keeps bringing on more horses, packing them in. You got to admire the way he handles them into the corral, they never even get a chance to fight him because he don't let them think about doing anything except what he wants.

All the time he's doing this, the sky is getting brighter and brighter and you can see the flames dancing on the clouds, and the air starts feeling thick and heavy and the soot comes out of the dark part of the night and settles over everything.

At first you can't feel the wind. You can hear this whistley far-off sound but you can't feel it. Then the heat starts to move and you realize *that's* what makes the wind. And you hate that wind! You hate it because the wind makes the fire and the fire makes the wind and you can't stop it.

When Rick gets every last horse in the corral he shuts up the gate and then he runs back to the main house. Mr. Jessup is busy rigging up the water pump so he can spray the horses down and keep them cool, and when he's not looking I sneak up to the top of the ridge so I can see what's going on – and maybe catch sight of Joe.

Up on the ridge the hot wind makes me squint so hard I can't see nothing but the heat. But I grit my teeth and I won't give in no matter what. Then my eyes go clear all of a sudden and the edge of the sky is blurred. I can see fire spreading like somebody's pouring it out of a bucket. I can see it leaking all over the dry grasslands and coming alive. There's every shimmery kind of colour in the fire all mixed up together, and if you watch it hard enough, you start to forget things. You watch that fire and it kind of hums inside your head and makes you feel wide awake and sleepy at the same time, and nothing matters but the fire. Then the wind starts singing high and sweet, and you just want to lie down and let the fire change you like it changes the grass. Change you from something dead and dry into something that lights up the world and blots out the stars and makes the wind sing so beautiful it hurts to hear it stop.

I guess a fire will make you stupid if you let it. Because I keep standing there like a fool, watching the fire come running right up the ridge at me, burning so quick and hot that clumps of dirt are exploding just ahead of the flames, and all I can think about is this: *What does Joe see inside the fire?* Can he hear that fire wind singing to him? Can he see the river inside the flames, or the fluttering wings? Can he feel the way it has to keep moving or die?

Then the flames come roaring up to the top of the ridge and the sparks fly up like birds on fire, and one of the spark-birds hits my hand and sizzles me awake.

I turn tail, then, and run like my rear end's been lit afire, which it almost has. I'm running down the back side of the ridge and waving my hands and shouting for Rick to look out for the horses, but the fire is making so much noise no one can hear me.

All of a sudden there's a *whooooosh!* that lifts me up and throws me down. The fire spits hot all around me and the air disappears and I don't dare breathe. Then it skips over me and I'm up and running again and Rick comes out of the smoke and grabs me.

"For heaven's sake, boy, don't run off again!" he says. "Come and help me with the horses!"

* * *

The horses have gone crazy with fear. There's better than two hundred animals jammed into the big corral, and they want to get out. They're all together, stampeding from one side to the other, and Rick is running with them on the other side of the rail, shouting them back and waving his hat. I go along with him, yelling and whistling, but I don't think the horses hear us. All they hear is the fire coming and that makes them want to find a way out.

The smoke turns so thick you can't see the horses but you can hear them. I can hear Lady inside the smoke but there's nothing I can do because the fear has took her over and she's not my pony now, she's part of two hundred stampeding horses and they're all thinking with the same brain.

Mr. Jessup comes out of the smoke with this old fire hose he's got hooked up to the water pump. Me and Rick help him with it as he sprays down the corral. The spray hits the hot sparks in the smoke and they sizzle and go out, but the horses don't pay no mind to the water or what it does to keep back the fire. Mr. Jessup keeps spraying at them until they're all shiny and wet and all the horses look like they're made of hot silver but they still don't care about anything except getting out.

I keep yelling for Lady but she won't listen, all she hears is the other horses. And the other horses are saying *run run run for your life* and Lady is running so hard I'm scared her heart will burst.

I'm waving for her to slow down when the horses get too close to the rail. This one horse stumbles and falls into the fence, and then all of them keep smashing and they bust a rail loose. A bunch of them break through the opening before Rick and Mr. Jessup can get the rail back up.

That's when she breaks free. I see Lady Luck come running out of that corral and she keeps on going into the smoke.

She's gone before you know it. Except I know where she's going even if I can't see all the way there. She's heading back to her stall, back to the stable.

That's where she's going, and the fire is going there, too.

25
The Fire Pony

I'm not thinking about anything but Lady when I run through those flames, and duck under the smoke, and slap at the burning cinders that go off like firecrackers in the air. Except I can't really tell what's the air and what's the burning part, and the stuff inside my lungs feels so hot and dry I want to stop breathing, it hurts so much.

The ground is burning and the sky is burning, and when I get there, the stable is burning, too. The way I find it is, I bump straight up against it, because I can't see with my eyes all teared up with cinders and soot. I have to feel my way along until I come to the side door, the one that leads into the tack room. I know it's the tack room because I can smell the leather getting hot.

The first thing I hear is Lady – the racket her hooves are making as she gallops in circles. At first I can't figure out where she's at, and then I find my way through the tack room into the main part of the barn. There she is, rearing up and kicking at the smoke.

"Lady!" I yell. "Come to me!"

But she won't. She's so busy trying to kick at the smoke she don't even know I'm there. She's kicking so high it's like she's decided to live on two legs like a human being, only she don't quite know how to do it.

I run back into the tack room and grab the first halter my hands see. Then I'm back with Lady, waving the halter and begging her to come back to earth.

I got to get that halter on her, that's the only way to lead her out.

We got to get out, and we got to do it quick! I can feel the heat rushing into the barn, and smoke is swirling up like the inside of an invisible chimney. It looks like thunderclouds are boiling up in the rafters, but really it's smoke and sparks.

I'm begging Lady to take the halter, but she's kicking at me like I'm part of the smoke. She's afraid of everything that moves and she don't know any better, but I can feel the *whoosh* of her front hooves missing me.

Now she's crashing around, and I have to fall down and roll under her belly to get away. I can smell how crazy she is. It smells like she's burning up inside.

All of a sudden there's a *whomp!* that makes the floor shake, and everything changes. A burning rafter crashes down from the roof and lands right in the way of leaving. Fire races along the beam, and the splintered part explodes like road flares. Before you know it, the fire is inside the barn. It's racing up the walls into the thundersmoke above.

"Lady!" I'm screaming. "Lady! Lady!"

And then I get this idea to climb up on the stalls. When Lady comes racing by, I throw myself down on her back. There's no saddles or halter to hang on to, so all I can do is grab hold of her mane. She don't try to buck me off, but she still won't stop.

There's only one way out now, and that's to jump clear over the beam that smashed through to the floor. But Lady shies away. I get her to run at it again, but she won't jump it. She's more afraid of that burning beam than she is of dying. I keep trying to turn her and make her jump, but she won't do it. The only thing she'll do is run in circles, and the fire is running in circles all around us. It's getting closer and closer.

I can't breathe much and that makes it feel slow and dreamy, no matter how fast everything is happening. I almost forget how I'm trying to get us out of the barn, and for a while it seems right, the way Lady and me are just running and running. It gets so dizzy and hard to breathe it makes me think I see the grandstands with all the people on fire, waving and cheering us like it don't hurt to burn up, like it's the best thing in the world and don't be afraid. Like the fire will make us win the race.

And then the smoke chokes me hard and the coughing wakes me up enough to know I don't want to win that race, and I'm smart enough to know that the fire lies because it wants you to stay inside, but you got to keep trying to get out.

Except there's no way out. The barn is burning up from the inside and there's no escape any more, even if Lady does jump the beam. We missed our chance, and now we have to stay inside the fire and do what it wants.

That's when I start breathing in the smoke on purpose, because I figure the smoke will make me go to sleep. I'd rather dream about the race than be inside the fire.

That's what I'm doing, breathing in a dream, when something big comes crashing through the wall.

* * *

They say that when me and Lady were inside the barn, Joe Dilly came out of the dark outside, all covered with soot except for the whites of his eyes. And when he heard I chased after my pony, he went into that big corral and found Showdown and got on his back and jumped the fence.

They say he rode through that fire like a wild man, whooping and hollering and waving his burned-up hat, and he was talking to Showdown and the horse heard him and went where Joe wanted him to go.

They say nobody ever rode a kill-crazy stallion bareback like Joe Dilly, leaping that wild horse through the running fire as they flew in and out of the smoke, in and out of the crazy light that came out of the flames.

Maybe Joe was telling Showdown what he saw in the fire. Maybe he was singing one of his stupid old songs. Maybe he was telling that horse how once he came out of nowhere in his old Ford pickup and found his beat-up little brother waiting, and how we became a family and lived on the road where nothing could catch us.

I don't know about none of that. All I know is that Joe and his black-eyed horse come crashing through the wall. They come crashing through and the burning wood smashes into burning pieces, and all of a sudden you can see the sky where the wall used to be.

I been breathing the smoke and I think it must be a dream, but then I hear Showdown scream out that he's hurt, and I can see where he broke both of his front legs coming through the wall. All of a sudden, there's Joe Dilly crawling up out of the wreckage, reaching his hand up to me.

I can tell he's hurt almost as bad as Showdown, and he's holding himself like his legs are broke, too, but that don't stop him grinning that cockeyed grin of his and saying, "How do, sports fans? Hot enough for you?"

"Joe, you came back!"

"Never mind about that," he says. "You better ride this pony on out of here while you still got the chance."

There's fire all around us and Lady won't listen to me. Joe strokes her face and breathes into her nose and he's touching her like he does. He talks real soft to her, so soft and low I can't make out what he's saying, but whatever it is, Lady listens. I can feel the fear go right out of her. She stops trembling and shying, like something cool and calm has got inside her. Like she don't know the world is burning up.

Joe takes his hands away from her. "Go on," he says. "She'll be okay now."

Right about then the cloud in the rafters turns inside out, and there's nothing but fire and light on the inside. It's so hot even the smoke is burning up. The wind gets inside with the fire and the whole place starts creaking and shaking.

"You come, too, Joe! Get on with me!"

He's shaking his head before I get the words out. "One man to a horse," he says. "She's too small for the both of us. Besides, I got to stay with Showdown. Don't worry, I'll be okay."

The stallion has quit fighting his busted legs and he's just lying here, waiting. You can see him watching Joe, like he thinks Joe can help him.

"You can't stay, Joe! Please!"

But Joe won't listen to me. He can hardly stand up, his own legs are stove in so bad, but he takes Lady's head in his hands and he kisses her and he says, "You're a fire pony now. You just take this boy and run right through whatever it is that spooks you, and you keep on running till it's cool and safe."

I tell him, "I won't go unless you come with us." Then the rafters start falling down, and Joe grins that grin of his and before I can stop him he slaps Lady on the rump with his burned-up hat and he shouts out *"Geronimo!"* and Lady takes off like a race just started.

She heads right through where Showdown broke the wall, and it happens so quick that when I look back all I can see of Joe Dilly is a flame that looks his size, and then I'm hanging on for dear life like he wants me to, and Lady keeps running, she's running faster than the fire and every time it licks us, she goes faster and faster and faster.

That filly runs past the corral, past all the other running horses, past where Rick and Mr. Jessup are fighting hard to find me, and she runs through the smoke and the sparks and the birds on fire. She keeps on running far out into the back country where there's nothing to burn and you can see where the stars are back in the sky, and the cactus look like soldiers with their hands cocked up to say hello.

She don't stop until it's cool and safe, just like Joe Dilly said when he made her into a fire pony.

26
As Good a Man as Any and Better than Most

That's all I remember about what happened that night. They say Sally Red Dawn found me sitting under a cactus and that I was so covered with soot she almost missed me. It turns out she's a nice lady after all, but I didn't know that then, and it's probably true I cursed her and wouldn't come back and Rick had to come and fetch me in his truck.

That was a year ago. Since then they built a brand-new stable where the old one burned, and new corrals, and Mr. Jessup put another cross up on the bluff because he says he don't care what anyone says, Joe Dilly was as good a man as any and better than most.

After a time I started going to school like Sally wanted, and wouldn't you know it's not so bad, even though I have trouble with my grammar, and I keep getting the words wrong.

I growed some, too, but not so much I can't ride every day after school.

All in all, the days are going pretty good lately, here at the Bar None, where everybody is always welcome. Sally helped with the papers so I can stay on and make it legal and never have to go back to a foster home. And Lady Luck came through all her troubles in the fire and she's stepping high and looking fine, and maybe we'll race her again come summer, if she feels like it. Mr. Jessup, he likes to say he's not getting any younger, but he's the same as always, and he still rides up straight, like he's walking in the saddle, and he still don't say much but just enough.

And me, I'll never ever forget all the things that happened, the good and the bad and the in-between, and how Joe Dilly tried so hard to fight the fire that burned inside him and kept making him do the wrong thing. And how he always came back to save me, for as long as he lived, and how he loved me like a brother and a father and a friend.

Look Beyond the Story...

What inspired you to write Fire Pony?

My wife Lynn and I drove across the country in the winter of 1993. It was the first time I'd seen the West, except for in an airplane or at a movie, and I was impressed with the awesome landscape, and I decided I wanted to write a story set in that landscape. Fires were raging across the West that year and it seemed natural to me that fire would be part of the story.

Did anyone in particular inspire you to become a writer? Parents? Teachers?

Both of my parents were avid readers. Both of them would've liked to have been writers. But, what really inspired me to become a writer was getting excited by the books I read. That inspired me. It's like if you're a kid and love to watch baseball, it would be natural that you would want to play baseball. It was a very natural thing for me to go from reading to writing.

As an adult, how are you able to get inside the head of a kid so well?

The short answer to that is that I vividly remember being short. I have a very keen recollection of being eleven and twelve years old, and I use my own memories of how I felt at the time to create the characters I'm writing today.

What is your favourite part of the writing process? Is it like any other job?

I don't think it's like any other job – sometimes it's easier, sometimes it's harder, but my favourite part is thinking up the stories. Sometimes the writing down part of it is like a regular job. But that's all part of the process. You have to work for anything good.

Do you have a favourite passage from one of your books?

I think that the chapter about the attack of the mountain lion in *Fire Pony* is one of the best things I've ever written. It's only six or seven pages, but it's very vivid.

What is the hardest part about writing a book?

The hardest part about writing is developing the necessary discipline – getting in the habit of writing every day, then learning to rewrite and improve upon your material. The art of rewriting and self-editing is what separates the pros from the amateurs.

Have you ever put aside a book for a long time before finishing it? If so, why?

The answer is yes I have. Usually because I got stuck in the middle of the story and didn't know how to finish it. I've found, however, that it's very difficult for me to go back and finish a story after I've put it aside for any length of time. So now I try to finish a story, no matter how difficult the writing is.

Out of all the characters in your books, is there one that has become your favourite? If so, who?

The character that is my favourite is always the character I'm writing about right now. But, to be honest, I have great affection for Maxwell Kane (who is in *Freak the Mighty*), because he's the one who got me into writing books for younger readers. He was the first character I wrote about.

Is there anything you wish you could change about any of your books?

It's always a temptation to go back and read your old material and see where improvements could be made.

But once a book is published, that's it. You have to go on to the next book. The only thing I'd change is the number of copies sold!

What do you mean when you say: "Imagination is a muscle — the more you use it, the stronger it gets"?

I mean that if you want to use your imagination, you have to practise with it. If you wanted to be good at basketball, you'd have to practise shooting baskets. If you want to use your imagination, if you want to be a writer or an artist, or do something creative for a living, you have to use your imagination. You have to use it every day. If you do, it'll get stronger and better, just like an athlete will get stronger and better.

Is there anything else you would like to say to your readers?

Yes. What I always say to my readers:
KEEP READING!!

About the Author
In his own words

"I started writing stories in sixth grade. But writing wasn't cool, like being good at sports, or being part of the in crowd, or winning fights on the playground. It wasn't a 'normal' activity, and like most kids that age, I desperately wanted to be 'normal'. So writing became my secret life.

"At the age of sixteen I completed a novel – a book-length series of stories about two characters. The narrator is a boy who admires his best friend, who is a kind of genius, and the gifted friend eventually dies a tragic death. The two buddies hang out in the basement and share a series of adventures. It was rejected. No surprise, actually, because I wasn't like the genius kid I was writing about. The book simply wasn't good enough to be published.

"Eleven years after I finished that first novel, I was still unpublished. But I was determined to make my living as an author. So I kept writing. In the meantime, I worked a variety of labouring jobs – longshoreman, carpenter, boat builder – and started a couple of businesses that went nowhere. Finally, I found a publisher for my genre novels, which were mostly mysteries and thrillers for grown-ups.

"After I had written more than a dozen adult genre novels, an editor I knew in New York asked me to write a mystery for young adults. I said I wasn't interested; but on my way home to Maine, I heard a voice in my head. It was the voice of Maxwell Kane, and he wanted to tell me the story of his little genius buddy. The voice in my head became *Freak the Mighty*, and much of it came directly out of the novel I had written as a sixteen year old.

"That insistent kid voice in my head has helped me reinvent myself as a writer. That voice is still talking, demanding that I write down his story. It was that voice that made me realize that I do, indeed, have stories to tell for sixth, seventh, and eighth graders – stories about spirited kids who find a way to triumph over adversity.

"How do you keep the voice coming? A good memory helps. I vividly remember my sixth-grade classroom. I remember what it smelled like, where I sat, what I could see out the window, and how I felt about things. Peel away my decrepit middle-aged exterior, and an important part of me is still twelve years old. It helps me when I sit down to write stories for kids.

"And here's where the Young Adult author gets the big payoff. If a kid enjoys a book, she or he *really* enjoys it. Kids read uncritically, in the best sense of the word. They care about how the story makes them feel. If a story makes any impression at all, they write to the author. Let me tell you, those letters are just wonderful. The vast majority of young readers speak to you straight from the heart. *I liked this part, it made me laugh. I liked that part, it made me cry.* That was the wonderful surprise, the something extra I never expected in my secret life as a writer. Letters from kids I've never met, but who speak to me with a clarity and personality that makes them leap from the page.

"I love getting these fresh, wonder-filled messages from kids. As a writer I'm convinced that encouraging children to write fiction, to hook into that marvellous machine called the imagination, has to be good for everyone. It's good for the teachers who see students bloom into writers under their tutelage. It's good for the kids, who learn that they can work the same kind of magic they find in books. It's good for all of us, because soon these kids are going to emerge as the next generation of authors – and there won't have to be any 'secret' about it."

Other books by Rodman Philbrick

Freak the Mighty

Max is used to people being scared of him and calling him stupid because he's big and slow and looks like his dad, Killer Kane. Kevin is used to people laughing at him and calling him Freak because he's a crippled kid. But when the two boys meet, they form an extraordinary friendship. With Freak's incredible intelligence and imagination, and Max's great physical strength, they make an unstoppable team. With Kevin riding high on Max's shoulders, they become Freak the Mighty.

"A small classic, funny-sad, page-turning and memorable... It celebrates language, loyalty and imagination, and leaves you smiling." *The Sunday Times*

An American Library Association Best Book for Young Adults
A Judy Lopez Memorial Award Honour Book

9780746087251   £5.99

Lobster Boy

Skiff Beaman needs a whole heap of money to fix up his family's fishing boat. His father won't help – he can't see further than the next can of beer since Skiff's mother died. But Skiff can still hear his mum telling him "Never give up." So he comes up with a crazy plan that will see him fight a great and dangerous battle against the sea.

"It's the pace, excitement and above all, the inspirational voice of this story that make it unputdownable." *The Scotsman*

9780746090824   £5.99

The Last Book in the Universe

The one good thing in Spaz's life is his little sister Bean. But Bean is dying. Spaz is determined to save her, but in a world devastated by an earthquake, and dominated by vicious gangs and mindprobes, nothing is easy. Plunging into dangerous territory, Spaz must trust in the wisdom of an old man to survive.

"Gritty, moving and provocative, this is a vivid and futuristic adventure." *tBkmag*

9780746090794   £5.99